UNDERSTANDING MODERN ART

Monica Bohm-Duchen and Janet Cook

Edited by Felicity Everett
Designed by Mary Cartwright
Picture research by Milly Trowbridge

Illustrated by David Gillingwater

Additional designs by John Russell

CONTENTS

ABOUT THIS BOOK

Modern art is something that bewilders and frustrates a lot of people. This book attempts to demystify it and help you judge modern works from a more informed viewpoint. Each double-page spread considers a major theme or issue in modern art, such as nature, or city life. Two or three works are examined in detail, and there are suggestions of other paintings or sculptures which you could look at.

Looking at works of art in a book is a poor substitute for seeing the real thing. Beside each work, there is information on which museum or gallery houses it. Although many of the works reproduced in this book are on permanent display, some of the "other works to look at" are not, due to limited space. Before you make a special trip to see a particular work, it is worth telephoning the gallery first to make sure that you won't have a wasted journey. On pages 56-59, you can find the addresses, telephone numbers and opening hours of most of the museums and galleries mentioned in this book.

Because the works reproduced on the following pages come from collections all over the world, you may not be able to see them all. So try to imagine what the work would look like in real life; in particular, its colour, texture and size. Look for the dimensions shown beside each work. The height is given first, then the width, then, for sculptures, the depth.

Dotted throughout the book, you will find cartoons which have been printed in newspapers and magazines over the past hundred years. As well as making you laugh, they often show how artists' work was received by their contemporaries.

For a quick summary of the aims and ideas of a movement, refer to the charts on pages 52-55. Technical terms are printed in **bold type** and explained in the glossary on page 62.

3

WHAT IS MODERN ART?

Many people are baffled when they go to an art gallery and see a splattered canvas given the same status as an "Old Master". The role of art in western culture has changed in the last hundred years. Technical skill and realism, predominant since the 15th century*, are now less relevant. Yet most people still regard such qualities as the hallmarks of good art.

Before modern art

The following subjects were the mainstay of "traditional" art:

1. Portraits. People have always wanted to have their likeness recorded for posterity, but only the rich could afford it.

2. Religion and mythology. Scenes from the Bible and from Greek and Roman legends provided colourful and morally instructive subject-matter.

3. Scenes of everyday life. As society became more and more democratic, demand grew for pictures which could be easily understood without a classical or religious education.

Anonymous Byzantine: Madonna and Child on a Curved Throne. c1200 Tempera on wood. 81.5 x 41.9cm (32¹/₈ x16¹/₂ in). National Gallery of Art, Washington, USA

Paolo Uccello: The Battle of San Romano. c1450. Tempera on wood. 181.6 x 320cm (5ft 11¹/₂in x10ft 6in). The National Gallery, London, England

4. Historical events. Those in power wanted to record important events, particularly when they were the heroes or victors.

5. Landscapes. Nostalgia for the unspoiled natural world grew as western society became more and more industrialized.

6. Still lifes. Artists sometimes painted objects for their symbolic qualities, but as often for their own sake.

Rachel Ruysch: Still Life with Snake. 1685-90. Oil on canvas. 52 x 40cm (20¹/₂ x15³/₄in). Ashmolean Museum, Oxford, England

● What changed?

The invention of photography in the 1830s encouraged artists to attempt even greater realism in their paintings in an effort to compete with it. But as the 19th century wore on, some artists began to question the need for art to refer to the outside world at all. This led to the development of **abstract art.**

A second factor was the decline of patronage - the system whereby the church, royalty and the aristocracy commissioned works of art. By the 19th century art dealers had begun to sell uncommissioned art to a wider public. This gave artists more freedom to paint what and how they liked.

● Modern art movements

As artists began to experiment with new styles and techniques, they gathered in groups to talk about their ideas. Artists with similar aims sometimes formed a movement (for example, Futurism). Apart from creating a sense of solidarity and confidence, the movements gave them authority; groups of artists tended to be taken more seriously than individuals.

● Avoiding "isms"

It is very tempting to pigeon-hole artists, according to the movement they were most associated with. But this ignores the fact that each artist is an individual, and every work of art unique. The knowledge, for example, that Dalí belonged to the Surrealist group when he painted the Persistence of Memory (see page 27) may help our understanding of the painting, but it is only one aspect of the work.

● The avant-garde

Deriving from "vanguard" (the leading unit in an army), this term refers to artists who defy the establishment. But yesterday's avant-garde often become today's mainstream, as new artists explore yet more radical ideas.

* The 15th century marked the beginning of a time of cultural rebirth in Europe known as the **Renaissance**.

Modern art on trial

" It isn't lifelike."

Even the most realistic work of art is just a visual illusion. Just consider what a strange thing it is to try to create the illusion of a three-dimensional scene by putting paint on a flat surface. Now that photos, film, T.V. and video can do the job so well, shouldn't painting be concerned with a different sort of reality?

"Anyone can do it."

Many people judge a work of art by the apparent technical skill of the artist. They look for features such as "correct" perspective and subtle shading, which create the illusion of three dimensions. But isn't evidence of an original mind just as important? In fact, many modern artists have felt that over-emphasizing technique can stifle the imagination.

" I can't understand it ."

There is never just one interpretation of a work of art. Your own personal response is as valid as a critic's, especially if you look carefully and think about what you see. Finding out about the artist and the context in which the work was produced can also help you to get more out of it.

London Laughs: Modern Rooms, Tate Gallery, "Willy! Did you do that?"

Evening News, Associated Newspapers Group Ltd. c1936 (Lee)

● Jackson Pollock's Yellow Islands

This painting is typical of the kind of art that is sharply criticized. It isn't remotely realistic, yet it has a number of striking characteristics:

1. The rhythmic pattern across the picture surface can conjure up different emotions in the viewer, just as music evokes different moods in the listener*.

2. The boldness and density of the marks on the canvas show the energy with which the artist has painted it.

3. Unlike most traditional works of art, it doesn't pretend to be anything other than a painting.

Jackson Pollock: Yellow Islands. 1952. 143.5 x 185.4cm (56in x 6ft 1in). Tate Gallery, London, England

4. Some people think it inspires the viewer to look beyond the world of recognizable objects, to a more spiritual or imaginative plane.

How he did it

Pollock was one of the first Action painters (see page 52). Instead of painting at an easel, he laid his canvas on the floor, then poured and dripped paint on to it. For this painting, he then stood the canvas upright, added more black paint, and let it run down the picture.

Jackson Pollock at work on an action painting.

His spatter is masterful, but his dribbles lack conviction.

New Yorker, 26 Dec. 1953 (Peter Arno c1953)

● The childish streak

When people say of a work of art "A five-year-old could do it", they usually mean it as criticism. Yet, the artist might well be pleased. Many have admired the spontaneity and intensity of art done by children, the insane, or people in primitive societies (such as parts of Africa or medieval Europe). A number have tried to emulate such qualities in their work. One of the best-known modern artists, Henri Matisse, said: "We must see all of life as if we were children."

* Many modern artists, Gauguin (see page 30) and Kandinsky (see page 31), for example, have believed that art, like music, should communicate on an intuitive level.

5

STILL LIFE

Still life painting is the depiction of one or more inanimate objects. As with landscape (see page 8), 17th century Dutch artists were the first to paint them for their own sake. Before that they were usually only used as props to make a scene more credible. Some artists painted still lifes primarily to show off their technique: others gave them a more symbolic dimension (see page 4 and below, right) or used them to express their states of mind*. But perhaps the key role of the still life in modern art has been as a focus for technical and stylistic experiments, as was the case with the Cubists.

Cézanne's Apples and Oranges

Cubism did not happen spontaneously. It was the result of a gradual process of change, of which Cézanne was one of the main instruments. Judged by the standards of realism and technical achievement which had existed since the **Renaissance**, this painting would surely rank as a failure. The plate isn't round and the bowl seems to have come out of a jelly mould. You see the apple on the plate from above and the oranges in the bowl from the side. But Cézanne wasn't interested in realism - he wanted to explore the visual and psychological effects of showing things from different angles simultaneously.

For most of his life, Cézanne's work was ignored by the art establishment. However, many members of the **avant-garde**, including Picasso, found him an inspiration. Yet when some of them went to pay homage to him, they discovered that Cézanne had become so accustomed to the indifference of the outside world that he didn't believe their praise was sincere.

Paul Cézanne: Still Life with Apples and Oranges. 1895-1900. Oil on canvas. 73 x 92cm ($28^{5}/_{8}$ x $36^{1}/_{2}$in). Musée d'Orsay, Paris, France

Cubism

When you think about it, the idea of portraying 3-dimensional objects on a 2-dimensional surface is rather a contradictory one. Inspired by African tribal art and Cézanne's pioneering work, Braque and Picasso explored this contradiction in their paintings, between 1907 and 1914. They felt that they were being both more honest and more realistic, by recognizing the problems in depicting the world two-dimensionally, than artists who tried to create an illusion of reality.

Which is nearer to the truth, the sketch on the left, or the Cubist-style wine glass on the right? Both are conventions.

Picasso and Braque used several devices to convey what they felt to be a more complex version of reality in their paintings. The main one was their rejection of single viewpoint **perspective**, which had dominated art since the Renaissance. Another involved the use of (often witty) verbal and visual clues to the meaning of their paintings - see above right.

Other works to look at

- James Ensor: The Ray. 1892. Musées Royaux des Beaux Arts de Belgique, Brussels, Belgium
- Pablo Picasso: Still Life with Chair Caning. 1912. Musée Picasso, Paris, France
- Juan Gris: The Sunblind. 1914. Tate Gallery, London, England
- Fernand Léger: Still Life with Beer Mug. 1921-2. Tate Gallery, London, England
- Joan Miró: Still Life with an Old Shoe. 1937. MoMA, New York, USA

* For example, the Miró and Ensor paintings listed in "Other works to look at".

Braque's Clarinet and Bottle of Rum on a Mantelpiece

Although this work looks almost abstract, by comparison with the Cézanne on the left, it not only contains recognizable objects, but also takes Cézanne's approach even further. Braque has deliberately chosen a very limited colour scheme to draw attention to his experiments with form.

• At the top of the large pyramid is a big rectangle with a smaller one on top of it. Does it look like a bottle to you? It is labelled RHU - the first three letters of *rhum*, the French word for rum.

• Jutting out behind the bottle is the clarinet, its sound holes shown from the side, but its endpiece seen from the back, almost as a circle.

• Can you spot the scroll-like shape, which represents the decorative support of the mantelpiece in the title?

• VALSE is French for waltz, and suggests a piece of sheet music.

Georges Braque: Clarinet and Bottle of Rum on a Mantelpiece. 1911. Oil on canvas. 87.6 x 60.3cm (34¹/₂ x 23³/₄in). Tate Gallery, London, England

Which way up?

About a third of the way down, there is a shape that resembles a nail. This was Braque's witty way of telling us which way up the painting goes. It also makes fun of conventional still lifes, which pretend to be real, by emphasizing that this is only a painting. Like the other objects, it is shown from various angles. Its shadow suggests lighting from the left, whereas the nail itself seems to be lit mainly from the right.

"I tell you, Herb, forty-nine people can't be wrong!"

London Opinion, Jan. 1953 (Bruce Cavalier)

O'Keeffe's Cow's Skull

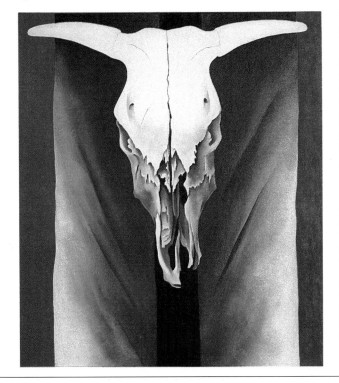

There is no doubting the subject of this painting. The skull is depicted realistically from a conventional single viewpoint. O'Keeffe was inspired by the many bleached animal bones she saw around her home in the New Mexican desert.

Do you think she just wanted to paint a skull as accurately as possible, or is there more to it than that? The skull's size and the lack of a realistic background give it a

Georgia O'Keeffe: Cow's Skull: Red, White and Blue. 1931. Oil on canvas. 101.3 x 91.1cm (39⁷/₈ x 35⁷/₈in). Metropolitan Museum of Art, New York, USA

haunting quality, so perhaps it symbolizes something. Skulls were often used in traditional still life as a reminder of man's mortality. Some see the positioning of the skull on the black strip as referring to Christ's crucifixion. The red areas could be said to evoke blood and, perhaps, the earth. The blue backdrop may symbolize the sky, and the diagonal creases in it, mountains. The use of red, white and blue (the colours of the American flag) may be ironic. O'Keeffe may have been satirizing the rather fanatical patriotism in much American painting of the 1930s.

7

NATURE

Artists have painted nature for centuries, but for a long time it served as a backdrop to more "important" subjects. 17th century Dutch artists were the first to paint landscapes for their own sake. Then, from the late 18th century, other European artists began to follow suit.

As Europe became more and more industrialized, art began to reflect a growing nostalgia for the old rural way of life. By the 20th century, though, artists were becoming much less conventional in the way they portrayed both landscape and nature in general.

● Monet's Waterlilies

Does this painting strike you as incompetent? You would be unlikely to mistake it for a photograph of a lily pond, such as the one shown below, but does that make it any less impressive? Perhaps, then, it may surprise you that some of the qualities which make this painting

Monet's lily pond at his home in Giverny, which is now open to the public*.

so evocative were the very ones for which Monet and his fellow Impressionists were ridiculed when they first exhibited (see below left).

The Impressionists usually painted outdoor scenes, on the spot, in front of their subject.

Impressionism

Named by a hostile critic, this first modern art movement rebelled against the Paris establishment who thought that scenes from history or the Bible were the noblest subjects for art. Critics, used to the near-photographic realism of most 19th century painting, thought the deliberate sketchiness of Impressionist works a sign of incompetence.

Policeman: "Lady, it would be unwise to enter!"

● Van Gogh's The Starry Night

How do you think van Gogh felt as he painted this nocturnal scene? The swirling sky, bright moon, flame-like trees and exploding stars contrast markedly with the orderly horizontal and vertical lines of the village below. Doesn't this suggest that the villagers are sleeping peacefully, unaware of the natural world in complete chaos around them? Van Gogh always had a strong sense of God's presence in nature and felt very small and insignificant in the scheme of things. Can you identify with him when you look at The Starry Night?

The "tragic painter"

Although he never achieved public recognition in his lifetime, van Gogh is now so famous that his tragic life story has been told in books, films and even in a pop song. The sensational aspects (such as his mental seizures and suicide) tend to be over-played. Many people see his work as evidence of the popular myth that madness and genius are two sides of the same coin. This can be misleading, because although many of his works convey great emotion, they were all painted when the artist was in control of his faculties.

Vincent van Gogh: The Starry Night. 1889. Oil on canvas. 73.6 x 92cm (29 x 36¼in). MoMA, New York, USA

They tried to capture a sense of the fleeting moment which resulted in a rather sketchy technique and the use of strong colour to convey the play of light in the open air. In fact, Waterlilies rejects the **plein air** (outdoor) principle of Impressionism. It was one of a series of vast paintings of the lily pond, done, not beside the pond, but in a specially constructed studio. By this time the Impressionists had split up and Monet was more concerned with expressing an almost mystical sense of communion with nature than with working spontaneously.

Claude Monet: Waterlilies. 1920. Oil on canvas. 2 of 3 sections 198 x 427cm (6ft 6in x 14ft). MoMA, New York, USA

Matisse's Snail

Do you think you would have guessed the subject of this picture, if it weren't given away in the title? Most people would probably think it was an abstract work. The snail may not be obvious straight away, but have a look at the photograph below, then back at the picture and you may well begin to see what Matisse was getting at. Starting with the green shape in the middle, the snail's shell spirals outwards, ending with the pale green square, bottom right. Can you spot the witty clue hidden at the top of the lilac shape?*

Henri Matisse: The Snail. 1953. Gouache on cut and pasted paper. 286.4 x 287cm (112³/₄ x113in). Tate Gallery, London, England

Other works to look at

- Paul Cézanne: La Montagne Ste. Victoire. c1886-8. Courtauld Inst. of Art, London, England

- Georges Seurat: Port-en-Bessin, Entrance to the Harbour. 1888. MoMA, New York, USA

- Jacob Epstein: Doves. c1913. Tate Gallery, London, England

- Emile Nolde: Tropical Sun. 1914. Ada and Emile Nolde Foundation, Seebull, Germany

- Paul Nash: We are Making a New World. 1918. Imperial War Museum, London, England

- Georgia O'Keeffe: Single Lily with Red. 1928. Whitney Museum of American Art, New York, USA

How he did it

In 1953, Matisse was over 80 and confined to bed through ill-health. From here, he instructed his assistants to paint large pieces of paper with gouache (an opaque water-colour paint) in colours of his choice. Matisse then cut shapes out of the paper. His assistants pinned them on to white paper, following his directions, and pasted them down.

* There is a tiny snail-like shape jutting out of it.

PEOPLE

The human figure has always been a favourite subject for artists but not all of them have tried to depict it realistically. Since the Renaissance, however, artists showed people looking, on the whole, like people.

Because most modern artists have been less concerned with realism, anatomical accuracy has become less important and the figure has been distorted in ways which have sometimes made it barely recognizable.

● De Kooning's Woman I

This is the first in a series of images of women painted by de Kooning in the early 1950s, which caused quite a stir when it was exhibited in 1953. It's easy to see why - it is a dramatically different portrayal of womanhood from the kind found in traditional art. Does it remind you of anything? What about those 50s "pin-ups", with their wide grins, big eyes and sexy figures? By exaggerating and distorting these features, de Kooning could be said to be parodying the ideal of womanhood which they represent.

Rita Hayworth was a popular pin-up at the time when de Kooning painted Woman I.

Willem de Kooning: Woman I. 1950-2. Oil on canvas. 193 x 147.3cm (6ft 3⁷/₈in x 4ft 10in). MoMA, New York, USA

Women and nature

The idea of women somehow belonging to the natural world is a very old theme in western culture. Both the earth mother and love goddess images stress woman's sexual and reproductive capacities and link them with the life force in nature. It is hard to tell whether de Kooning's mocking references to these stereotypes are made in a spirit of solidarity with women or of hostility towards them.

Moore's Recumbent Figure (right) refers to the same stereotypes as Woman I, yet seems to project a much more sympathetic image of womanhood.

The sheer size of Woman I, and her stalwart pose, on the other hand, are suggestive of a less glamorous, but equally familiar stereotype, the "earth mother" (woman as a symbol of fertility and nurturing). Again, instead of emphasizing the positive aspects of this role model, the artist gives us a fearsome parody.

De Kooning regarded this painting as comic, which may add weight to the theory that he was mocking the tradition of the ideal woman. Like Moore, he identified women with nature, saying that a woman's shape reminded him of "a landscape - with arms like lanes and a body of hills and fields, all brought close up to the surface, like a panorama squeezed together".

A slapdash painting?

Although the painting looks slapdash, de Kooning produced numerous preparatory drawings, and worked on the canvas for almost two years. Like many modern artists, he rejected the traditional need to demonstrate his technical skill in an obvious way (for example through minute detail, or the use of correct **perspective**).

Although de Kooning was a key member of the Abstract Expressionist group, his occasional choice of **figurative** subject-matter set him apart from the rest of the group. However, the apparently random application of paint in Woman I is characteristic of all his mature work.

Other works to look at

• Pablo Picasso: Les Demoiselles d'Avignon. 1907. MoMA, New York, USA

• Mikhail Larionov: Soldier on Horseback. c1911. Tate Gallery, London, England

• Ludwig Kirchner: Five Women on the Street. 1913. Wallraf-Richartz Museum, Cologne, Germany

• William Roberts: The Cinema. 1920. Tate Gallery, London, England

• Paul Klee: Drummer. 1940. Klee-Stiftung, Kunstmuseum, Bern, Switzerland

● Moore's Recumbent Figure

It is not immediately obvious that the figure in this sculpture is female. The title tells us about its pose, but not its gender. However, "reading" the sculpture as recumbent (or reclining) helps us to relate it to the human form. The head and neck are seen side-on and below them are two lumps which can only be breasts, so the figure must indeed be a woman, leaning on her elbows (bottom left) with one knee raised (top right).

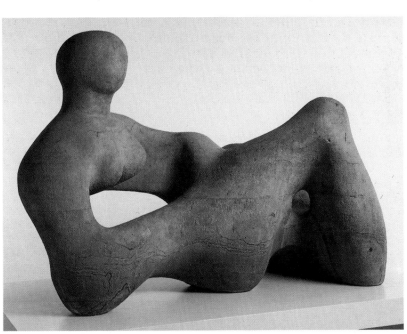

Henry Moore: Recumbent Figure. 1938. Green hornton stone. 88.9 x 132.7 x 73.7cm (35 x 52¼ x 29in). Tate Gallery, London, England

Punch, 27 June 1951

"That reminds me, dear - did you remember the sandwiches?"

The image of a reclining female figure dates back to the **Renaissance**, when Venus, the Roman goddess of love, was often shown in that pose. What other associations does the sculpture have? The stomach (a hole) links the figure with the space around it. The fusion of the arms with the torso creates a flowing shape, emphasized by naturally-occurring wavy lines on the surface*. Isn't the overall effect evocative of potholes and caves, eroded by the natural forces of wind and water?

● Miró's Person Throwing a Stone at a Bird

Without the title of this painting to help decipher it, it would be hard to say for certain what is going on. The large white figure on the right (the person?) is divided into four distinct parts; a head, a neck, a body and a leg with a huge foot and splayed toes. The stone is surely the black and white object slightly to the left of centre. This would make the black diagonal across the figure, represent the arm that has thrown it, and suggests that the curved, dotted line represents the path the stone has travelled. The bird is easy enough to spot, with its blue head,

Joan Miró: Person Throwing a Stone at a Bird. 1926. Oil on canvas. 73 x 92cm (28³/₄ x 36¹/₄in). MoMA, New York, USA

red crest, curved wings and tail feathers.

Miró was an important member of the Surrealist group (see page 26), which he joined because of his interest in dreams and the subconscious. He said *"...as I paint, the picture begins to ... suggest itself, under my brush...The first stage is free, unconscious... (but) the second stage is carefully calculated."*

What does this painting actually *mean*? On one level it seems like a simple comment on human violence against nature. But in other pictures by Miró birds symbolize the power of the imagination, so perhaps the bird in this picture is a symbolic *extension* of the person. How might this affect the meaning of the painting?

* These are a result of Moore's technique of carving spontaneously, without preliminary studies, to allow the materials an active role in the making of the sculpture.

EMOTIONS

In a realistic painting or sculpture, emotion is expressed mainly through people's poses and expressions; although composition and colour also play a role. But in works of art which exaggerate or distort their subjects, or abstract works which *have* no easily identifiable subject, colour and composition are crucial to our understanding and appreciation. By responding to these visual prompts on an instinctive level we can often sense the mood of even the most obscure paintings and sculptures.

● Munch's The Scream

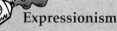

What emotion do you think this man is feeling? Surely his screaming mouth and anguished expression convey sheer terror. The face itself has the shape and hollow features of a skull, perhaps suggesting a fear of (or is it a wish for?) death. The two figures approaching from the end of the pier add to the general mood of menace.

What effect has the artist achieved by painting the land, sky and water around the figure as dramatic, swirling shapes in unnatural colours? Don't you think it adds to the impression that this man's world is in total turmoil?

Edvard Munch: The Scream. 1893. Oil on cardboard. 91 x 73.5cm (35⁷/₈ x 28⁷/₈in). National Gallery, Oslo, Norway

A troubled mind

This is what Munch wrote about the painting:

"One evening, I was walking along a path, the city was on one side, and the fjord below. I felt tired and ill. I stopped and looked out over the fjord - the sun was setting, and the clouds turning blood-red. I sensed a scream passing through nature; it seemed to me that I heard the scream. I painted this picture, painted the clouds as actual blood. The colour shrieked. This became The Scream."

Munch was dogged by psychological problems all his life and The Scream was one of a series of powerful images painted between 1889 and 1909, partly to work them through. Munch called the series The Frieze of Life.

Expressionism

This term is sometimes used to describe the way many western artists from the late 19th century onwards have deliberately distorted subject-matter, form and colour to express their (often unhappy) states of mind. More often it refers to two early 20th century art movements based in Germany: Die Brücke (The Bridge), and Der Blaue Reiter (The Blue Rider) and one based in France, les Fauves (The Wild Beasts).

More Severe Punishments. Prosecution: "I submit that the criminal, in order to make his punishment more severe, should have modern pictures hung in his cell."

Fliegende Blätter, 2 Dec. 1898 (A. Roeseler)

Other works to look at

- Walter Sickert: Ennui. c1913-14. Tate Gallery, London, England
- Pablo Picasso: The Three Dancers. 1925. Tate Gallery, London, England
- Chaïm Soutine: Pageboy at Maxim's. 1927. Albright-Knox Art Gallery, Buffalo, NY, USA
- Arshile Gorky: Agony. 1947. MoMA, New York, USA

● Chagall's Birthday

Though this painting, like the one by Munch, uses distortion and bold colour to convey intense feeling, they could scarcely be more different in effect. The colours used are warm and bright and the kissing couple dominate the space, defying the laws of gravity and anatomy. These are hallmarks of Chagall's work - he believed that the world of the imagination and emotions was more real than "real" life. Think of the metaphors we use to describe being in love - "over the moon", "on cloud nine", "head-over-heels". Does Chagall's composition seem to make more sense now?

Marc Chagall: Birthday. 1915. Oil on cardboard. 80.5 x 99.5cm (31 x 39in). MoMA, New York, USA

Chagall in love

Chagall met his future wife, Bella Rosenfeld, in 1909. In her memoirs, Bella recalled how she visited him on his birthday, carrying food and flowers in embroidered shawls. They draped the shawls around the room, and Chagall began to paint. This is how Bella described the atmosphere that day: "*Spurts of red, blue, white, black...suddenly you tear me from the earth, you yourself take off from one foot... You rise, you stretch your limbs, you float up to the ceiling. Your head turns about and you make mine turn... You brush my ear and murmur...*"

Marc and Bella Chagall ▶

● Lehmbruck's Fallen Man

What aspect of this figure do you think conveys his emotions? We can't see his face, and except for the handle of a broken sword in his hand, there is no context to suggest how he might be feeling. It is surely his pose which expresses, all too effectively, his mood of despair. His whole body is directed downwards, as if to sink into the earth.

Lehmbruck has simplified and elongated the forms of the body and exaggerated the limpness of the limbs so as to emphasize the man's vulnerability.

Lehmbruck made this sculpture soon after the start of the First World War. It aroused great hostility amongst his fellow Germans for its apparent defeatism. Although he did not fight in the First World War himself, Lehmbruck was deeply depressed by it. A year after it ended, he committed suicide, aged only 38.

Wilhelm Lehmbruck: Fallen Man (Beaten Man/Dying Warrior). 1915-16. Stone cast. 78 x 240 x 82cm (31in x 7ft 11in x 32in). Staatsgalerie Moderner Kunst, Munich, Germany

THE ARTIST'S MODEL

Today the term "model" applied to art and photography has a slightly sleazy ring to it. We tend to assume immediately that the model is female, and probably naked; that the artist (and perhaps also the viewer) is male. Yet until the early 19th century models were as often male as female, largely because of the fashion for "heroic" subject-matter featuring muscular, partially-clad men. What's more, both modern and traditional art abound with images of clothed figures - male and female, young and old, many of which have been based on live models who do not conform to the stereotype.

● Picasso's Painter and Model

Pablo Picasso: Painter and Model. 1928. Oil on canvas. 130 x 163cm (51⅛ x 64¼in). MoMA, New York, USA

In most of his paintings of women, Picasso showed them either as passive and sexually provocative, or as aggressive and threatening. Yet it is hard enough even to pick out the woman here, let alone characterize her. So maybe this work deals with the relationship between art and life, rather than that between artist and model.

Of the three shapes in the painting which resemble people, the most likely candidate for the artist is surely the one on the right, whose head is shown as a large grey and black oval. He is sitting on a yellow and white chair holding a kidney-shaped palette and some kind of implement. In front of him, an easel holds a canvas on which is drawn a profile. This drawing looks more realistic than the figures on either side of it (the model is the figure with three eyes, to the left of this). Could Picasso therefore be suggesting that the only real thing is the painting itself?

The life of an artist's model

The job of modelling was tough and far from glamorous. It involved sitting still for a long time, often in an awkward position. The studios were often poorly heated and ventilated, and little attention was paid to the models' comfort.

Modelling, especially in the nude, was frowned upon. People assumed that female models were sexually available to the artists.

Punch, 25 Feb, 1948 (Starke)

"Miss Angelo is sorry she is feeling worse and cannot come today."

About self-portraits

Many artists have used themselves as models, further complicating the artist/model relationship. Expressionist painters, such as van Gogh, painted many self-portraits. This may be because artists who strive to express their innermost feelings are, of necessity, self-absorbed. Female artists also tend to favour self-portraits, partly perhaps, because of their sensitivity to the model's lowly status compared to that of the artist. They also use self-portraits to express their personal feelings and frustrations.

Other works to look at

• Vincent van Gogh: Portrait of the Artist with Severed Ear. 1889. Courtauld Institute Galleries, London, England

• Ludwig Kirchner: Self-Portrait with Model, 1909-10. Kunsthalle, Hamburg, Germany

• Egon Schiele: Standing Male Nude (Self-Portrait). 1910. Albertina, Vienna, Austria

• Laura Knight: Self-Portrait. 1913. National Portrait Gallery, London, England

• Henri Matisse: The Painter in his Studio. 1917. Musée Nationale d'Art Moderne, Centre Georges Pompidou, Paris, France

Kahlo's The Two Fridas

Why should this artist have painted two versions of herself? In one, her bodice and heart are torn open but in the other they remain whole. Who is the child in the portrait she is holding? From it runs a long vein, like an umbilical cord, that twists around her arm, through her heart, encircles the other Frida's neck, enters her broken heart and ends on her lap. This might lead you to think that Frida is mourning her own dead child. Actually this picture is almost certainly about her traumatic divorce from her husband, Diego Rivera. She first invented her imaginary twin to work through her distress when she had polio at the age of six. Here, the heartbroken Frida wears a Victorian dress; the other a Mexican skirt and blouse (Kahlo was part Mexican Indian and part European). The child in the picture is Rivera, but the reference may be to a baby she lost in an earlier miscarriage, as well as to her lost husband.

Frida Kahlo and Diego Rivera in happier times.

The Frida Kahlo Museum
Kahlo was previously known mainly for her association with fellow artist Diego Rivera. However she has recently received considerable critical acclaim in her own right.

The house in Mexico City in which Kahlo was born, lived and died is now open to the public. It houses the Frida Kahlo Museum containing many of her paintings and mementoes. There are details of the museum on page 58.

Frida Kahlo: The Two Fridas. 1939. Oil on canvas. 170.2 x 170.2cm (67 x 67in). Museo de Arte Moderno, Mexico City, Mexico

Seurat's The Models

In the picture on the left, Seurat has given his models a dignity and chasteness usually denied them. By posing them in front of one of his own earlier paintings, Sunday Afternoon on the Island of La Grande Jatte, he contrasts a scene of leisure (in La Grande Jatte) with one of work (in his studio). The models' discarded clothes resemble those worn by the figures in the painting behind them, which could well be a wry comment on the private life of the French middle classes. So perhaps the models' nudity is meant to be ironic, rather than titillating.

Georges Seurat: Les Poseuses (The Models). 1888. Oil on canvas. 39.4 x 48.9cm (15¼ x 18¾in). Berggruen Collection, on loan until 1996 to the National Gallery, London, England

CITY LIFE

When European towns and cities began to expand during the Industrial Revolution (c1750-1850), people flocked to them in search of work. Factories and mills encroached on woods and fields; houses and tenements sprawled out from around the new work places.

Most artists were slow to reflect the changing scene in their work, continuing instead to portray idealized country scenes*. As time went on, the changing landscape became harder to ignore, and gradually more artists turned their attention to it. Some emphasized negative aspects, such as overcrowding and loneliness; others were excited by mechanization and the pace of urban life.

Fritz Lang's film Metropolis (1927) conveyed the surreal atmosphere of automated urban life.

● Delaunay's Eiffel Tower

Would you recognize this as the Eiffel Tower? Very likely you would. Even if you haven't seen the real thing, you have probably seen pictures of it in books, or on television, and in spite of the unusual composition of the painting, the distinctive architecture is still obvious. In 1889 when the tower was built it caused great controversy - some considered it an exciting feat of engineering, others thought it a monstrosity. Do you think Delaunay's attitude to it comes across in this painting?

Influenced by his friends Picasso and Braque, Delaunay used the Cubist device of depicting an object from several viewpoints at once.

Robert Delaunay: Eiffel Tower. 1910. Oil on canvas. 195 x 129cm (6ft 4³/₄in x 4ft 2³/₄ in). Kunstmuseum, Basel, Switzerland

Instead of applying this mainly to still life (see pages 6-7), as its pioneers did, Delaunay used it (as here) to convey the dynamism of city life. What effect do you think he has achieved by its use? The tower looks more dramatic and precarious than it would if it were painted realistically. So perhaps, in a sense, it is truer to life, as that is how the Eiffel Tower must have seemed to many Parisians at the turn of the century.

A room with a view

The Eiffel Tower appears in a lot of Delaunay's work. In 1910, a writer-friend of his, Blaise Cendrars, was convalescing in a hotel room which happened to have a magnificent view of the Eiffel Tower. Concerned for his friend, Delaunay visited him every day, and took the opportunity, while he was there, of sketching the view.

◀ **The real Eiffel Tower**

Other works to look at
- André Derain: The Pool of London. 1906. Tate Gallery, London, England
- Gino Severini: Suburban Train Arriving in Paris. 1915. Tate Gallery, London, England
- Edward Hopper: Nighthawks. 1942. Art Institute of Chicago, Chicago, USA
- Piet Mondrian: Broadway Boogie-Woogie. 1942-3. MoMA, New York, USA

* You can find out about the different ways in which artists dealt with the natural world on pages 8-9.

Giacometti's City Square

What impression of city life does this sculpture convey? Although you can tell the men from the women, there is little else to distinguish one figure from another. Doesn't this, and their strange, elongated shapes, give the impression that they are de-humanized and isolated? Perhaps this is Giacometti's sad commentary on the way city dwellers hurry past each other in a busy street or square, without communicating in any but the most superficial way.

How he did it

Giacometti built up his figures in plaster on a wire frame, then cast them in bronze. They are always abnormally tall and thin, possibly inspired by photographs of holocaust* victims.

Alberto Giacometti: City Square. 1948-9. Bronze. Each figure, 12.5-15.5cm (5-6in) high. Peggy Guggenheim Collection, Venice, Italy

Dubuffet's Business Prospers

What strikes you about this painting? That a child of five could have done it, perhaps? This would not have dismayed Dubuffet who championed the art of children, the insane and the self-taught. He admired its spontaneity and honesty and tried to capture these qualities in his own work. Hence the figures and buildings shown from different angles; some upright, some upside-down and all of them flattened. The result looks like a hectic jumble of patterns, scattered with graffiti. Although this seems livelier and more colourful than City Square, the people are separated by cell-like structures. Could this be Dubuffet's way of conveying their isolation from one another? In his graffiti-like shop signs (some of which are translated right), Dubuffet is satirizing the greed, dishonesty and hypocrisy encouraged by urban living:

Grotesque Bank

At the Funereal Smile

At the Sign of the Thief

The Short-Weight Shop

The Ministry of Greasy Paws

About graffiti

"Graffiti" means "little scratches" in Italian. Its modern meaning describes anything scribbled or sprayed on to a surface in a public space. Graffiti is often found on the walls of stations, public toilets and so on. Some see it as vandalism; others as a creative art form. A number of New York subway graffiti artists have recently become almost cult figures in the international art world.

Jean Dubuffet: Business Prospers. 1961. Oil on canvas. 165 x 218.4cm (5ft 5in x 7ft 2in). MoMA, New York, USA

* The term holocaust refers to the mass extermination by the Nazis of "undesirables" (in particular the Jews).

MOVEMENT

Speed is a key feature of modern life. Artistic groups such as the Vorticists (see page 24) and the Futurists (see below), were inspired by the dynamism of the machine age to try to capture a sense of movement in their work.

Since then, other artists, such as Alexander Calder and Jean Tinguely (see "Other works to look at") have literally made their art move; others, like Bridget Riley (see opposite) have made it appear to move.

(see page 24)

Other works to look at

- Umberto Boccioni: States of Mind: The Farewells: Those Who Go, Those Who Stay. 1911. MoMA, New York, USA

- Marcel Duchamp: Nude Descending a Staircase. 1912. Philadelphia Museum of Art, Philadelphia, USA

- Alexander Calder: Little Red Under Blue. 1947. Fogg Art Museum, Harvard University, Cambridge, Massachusetts, USA

- Jean Tinguely: Painting Machine or Metamatic. 1961. Stedelijk Museum, Amsterdam, Holland

Balla's Dynamism of a Dog on a Leash

Giacomo Balla: Dynamism of a Dog on a Leash. 1912. Oil on canvas. 91 x 110.5cm (35³/₄ x 43³/₈in). Albright-Knox Art Gallery, Buffalo, USA

From the **Renaissance** onwards, the conventional way in which artists tried to capture objects and people in motion was to fix them in one position, from one viewpoint, at one moment in time (see the Uccello on page 4 for example). Here, inspired by the photographic experiments of the French scientist Marey (see right), Balla defies tradition and shows successive movements at once. This technique was often applied by Balla and his fellow Futurists to convey a sense of awesome speed in pictures of machines and city life. Here, applied to a small dog, the effect is comic.

This photograph by Etienne-Jules Marey shows the photographic technique which Balla's painting imitates.

Futurism

Futurism emerged in northern Italy just before the First World War. Its founders celebrated contemporary urban life, and rejected artistic tradition. In their first manifesto (1908), they said "... *the splendour of the world has been enriched with a new form of beauty, the beauty of speed. A racing-car adorned with great pipes like serpents with explosive breath... is more beautiful than the Victory of Samothrace.*"

▲
A 1908 racing car of the type which (in motion) inspired the bold claims of the Futurists' manifesto.

◄ The Victory of Samothrace, a famous ancient Greek statue in the Louvre, Paris.

The Futurists went on to publish many aggressive manifestos; in one, they even demanded that all museums and libraries be demolished. They also staged events designed to shock the middle classes. The Dadaists, a few years later, and the performance artists of the 1960s, were also to adopt this tactic. Some of the Futurists were militaristic, and later supported Mussolini*, which has somewhat discredited the movement.

* Mussolini was the Fascist leader of Italy from 1922-1943

Riley's Fall

This painting, even more than the one by Balla, seems to move before our eyes. Why do you think it is called Fall? Is it because the wavy lines ripple down the canvas like a waterfall? Or perhaps because the long curves, gradually converging near the base of the painting, draw the eye downwards. Doesn't this evoke a falling sensation?

Riley's inspiration
One of the best-known Op artists, Riley was originally inspired by Pointillism*. This was a technique of the late 19th century whereby an image was created using hundreds of tiny dabs of paint. Viewed close up, the dots would not make sense (like a colour T.V. screen), but from a distance, a clearer picture would emerge.

Bridget Riley: Fall. 1963. Emulsion on board. 141 x 140.3cm (55$\frac{1}{2}$ x 55$\frac{1}{4}$in). Tate Gallery, London, England

Op art

Op art (short for Optical art) flourished in the late 1950s and 1960s. Most Op artists worked out their geometrical images carefully in advance, using scientific theories to make them appear to move. The result is unusual in art, in that it actually evokes a *physical* response, not just an emotional or psychological one.

Op art became a very trendy movement and had a big influence on fashion.

Two examples of 60s fashions based on Riley's designs.

Gertler's The Merry-Go-Round

Gertler was a contemporary of the Futurists, yet here we get a contrasting view of the same era. This painting can also be seen as a product of the machine age; look at the men in uniform – could the merry-go-round symbolize the war machine? Using the traditional fixed viewpoint, Gertler evokes movement not only by blurring the edges of the canopy and the horses' legs, but also by the fixed screams of horror on the riders' faces, which suggest that they can never dismount. Don't you think the garish colours and claustrophobic composition of the painting add to its nightmarish feel?

Why did he paint it?
Gertler didn't actually fight in the First World War himself, but many of his friends did, so his horror must have been keenly felt. Another, more personal explanation for the unease expressed in the painting may be that Gertler's family were poor Jewish immigrants living in the east end of London. By 1916, he had turned his back on his roots and was moving in fashionable circles. His letters reveal mixed feelings about this, and a sense that he no longer belonged anywhere.

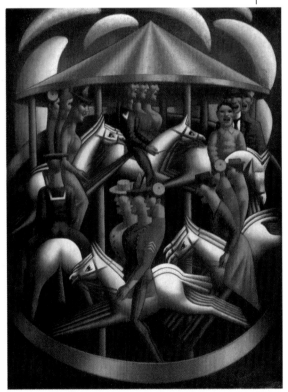

Mark Gertler: The Merry-Go-Round. 1916. Oil on canvas. 189.2 x 142.2cm (74$\frac{1}{2}$ x 56in). Tate Gallery, London, England

* Seurat's The Models on page 15 is an example of a Pointillist painting.

POLITICS

Although many people regard art and politics as quite separate areas of life, a number of artists have seen their work as political. Some opposed a repressive or corrupt régime; others supported a régime which they believed to be the best thing for their country and the world. These pages deal with the former, and the next two pages (entitled "Propaganda") deal with the latter. As you will see, artists who challenge the political status quo often use satire, caricature and exaggeration to convey their message.

● Blume's Eternal City

If you didn't know anything about the background to this painting, you might easily mistake it for a stage set. As in Dalí's paintings (see page 27), the realistic style - which imitates the Flemish and Italian **Old Masters** and perhaps, here, also Dalí's own work - doesn't seem to suit the surreal subject-matter. The grotesque jack-in-the-box in the middle of the painting seems particularly incongruous. Yet when you know that it is actually a caricature of Mussolini, Italy's Fascist leader in the 1930s, it may well provide the key to understanding the whole painting.

Blume was an American who spent a few months in Rome in 1932 and 1933. He was very disturbed by his visit which was the inspiration behind this nightmarish painting. In it he combined things he actually saw in Italy (such as a papier mâché sculpture of Mussolini, various churches and famous Roman remains) with a symbolic cast of characters and storyline.

All around Mussolini are signs of

Peter Blume: The Eternal City. 1934-7. Oil on composition board. 86.4 x 121.7cm (34 x 47⁷/₈in). MoMA, New York, USA

corruption. In the foreground, a smartly-dressed business man and a blackshirt (see left) leer up at their leader from the catacombs (ancient Roman burial chambers); a crippled beggar looks on, pathetically. In the background, a huge army seems about to crush a fearful band of civilians. The shrine on the left is based on a real shrine which Blume saw when he visited San Marco church, Florence. It shows Christ, surrounded by symbols of human vanity and power, such as jewels and swords. Surely this is meant to imply corruption in the church too? As with Grosz's work (see right), the title is ironic. The Eternal City is another name for Rome. In this painting, Blume is despairing at the city's political fate.

Blackshirts were members of the Italian Fascist party before and during the Second World War.

> ## Other works to look at
>
> ● Otto Dix: Big City. Triptych. 1927-8. Stuttgart Staatsgalerie, Stuttgart, Germany
>
> ● Jack Levine: Election Night. 1954. MoMA, New York, USA
>
> ● Renato Guttoso: The Discussion. 1959-60. Tate Gallery, London, England
>
> ● Hans Haacke: Metromobiltan. 1985. Musée Nationale d'Art Moderne, Centre Georges Pompidou, Paris, France

Golub's Mercenaries

Does this painting criticize a specific government or power? It shows soldiers wearing modern clothes and holding contemporary weapons, but they cannot be identified as belonging to any particular army. So we are at a loss to know what cause they are fighting for. Perhaps this is Golub's point. As mercenaries, these men do not care on whose side they fight, as long as they get paid for it. Golub said *"There is a near universal history of the use of violence as social practice"*, and it seems to be this fact, rather than any one régime, which he is criticizing in this picture.

This is one of a series of paintings in which Golub explores the relationship between violence, power

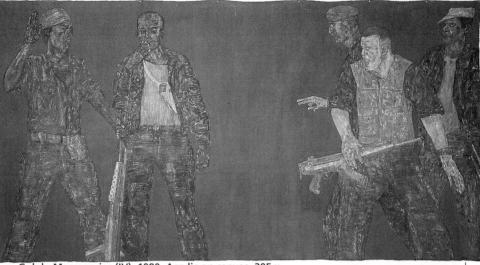

Leon Golub: Mercenaries (IV). 1980. Acrylic on canvas. 305 x 584cm (10ft x 19ft 2in). Saatchi Collection, London, England

and sadism (sexual pleasure gained from hurting others). Here, there is also a racially charged antagonism between the black man (far left) and the white man (right). Golub wants us to be repelled by the

men, yet their dramatic poses, the rich background colour and the painting's sheer size, have a mesmerizing effect, drawing us in almost in spite of ourselves.

Leon Golub working on Mercenaries.

Grosz' Pillars of Society

Don't these "pillars of society" all look either foolish, or wicked, or both? Germans of the 1920s would have known them well. The man with a Nazi swastika on his tie is an "old boy" of a student social club. He is holding a beer mug and a sword (members drank a lot at these clubs and also duelled to protect their honour). Behind him, the man with a chamberpot on his head is Hugenberg, a powerful press baron of the time. The fat man holding an old German imperial flag and a sign saying "Socialism is work" is meant to be a typical conservative politician - Grosz has cut off the top of his head to reveal a pile of excrement instead of brains. At the back, an army officer holds a bloody sword and a clergyman stupidly blesses everything in sight including a burning house. If these men are the pillars of society, Grosz appears to

be saying, then God help society!

Grosz was a Communist and social critic, and this painting is attacking the very structure of the German state. At the time, the country was being governed by the Weimar Republic which had replaced the Empire of Kaiser Wilhelm II at the end of the First World War. Grosz had experienced the horrors of that war at first hand and was dismayed that it had only served to strengthen Germany's commitment to nationalism and militarism - hence the swastika reference in the painting. Grosz soon became active in the Berlin Dada group - a politically active off-shoot of the international Dada movement (see page 32).

George Grosz: Pillars of Society. 1926. Oil on canvas. 200 x 108cm (78¾ x 42½in). Staatliche Museum Preussicher Kulturbesitz, Nationgalerie, Berlin, Germany

PROPAGANDA

Propaganda is information put out by a group of people with a common aim, to win over others. Propagandists have often used art as a tool, whether to illustrate a slogan, or put across a more subtle message. Ironically, the two most notorious political movements of the 20th century, Russian Communism and German Fascism, were at opposite ends of the political spectrum, yet used very similar artistic styles to win support.

● Lissitzky's Beat the Whites with the Red Wedge

Many artists who supported the Russian Revolution of 1917 promoted it in their art; some became members of the Constructivist movement (see right). Lissitzky called his abstract paintings *prouns*, which is Russian for "towards a new art". Even though this street poster is abstract, it has a strong symbolic message. The red wedge (Communism) is breaking into the white circle (white Russia, or non-Communism). In other words, the Communist revolutionaries are beating the old political system. The words reinforce the message, translating from left to right as "wedge", "red", "beat" and "whites". Would this style of propaganda have influenced you?

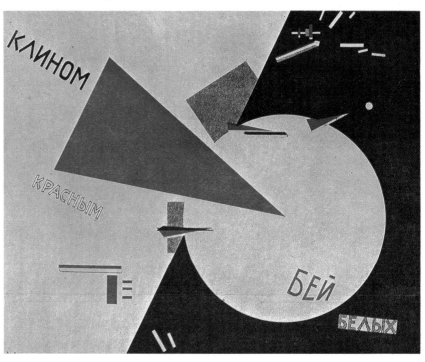

El Lissitzky: Beat the Whites with the Red Wedge. 1919-20. Poster. Ink on paper. 48 x 69cm (19 x 27in). Lenin Library, Moscow, USSR

● Moor's Have you volunteered?

This poster is promoting the same cause as the one by Lissitzky, but in a style more typical of propaganda images generally. Do you think it is more or less persuasive? The main figure represents the Red Army (the Communists) and the smoking factories symbolize the forces of industry and the working class. Why do you think Moor used a relatively realistic style for the figure? The challenging eyes and pointing finger are surely meant to make the people who haven't volunteered feel guilty. The same device was used in a British army recruitment poster of 1915, featuring Lord Kitchener. Moor's poster was produced in just one night. 45,000 copies were printed and distributed throughout Russia.

Soviet Socialist Realism

Perhaps not surprisingly, it was Moor's style of propaganda that the Soviet régime favoured in the end, not just for posters, but for paintings as well. Numerous pictures were produced of heroic soldiers, factory workers, peasants and their leaders (in particular, Lenin and Stalin). Although apparently realistic, these images were actually highly idealized and often melodramatic, working as an effective form of propaganda. This kind of art became known as Soviet Socialist Realism.

Dimitri Moor: Have you volunteered?. 1920. Lithograph. 106.4 x 71.2cm (42 x 28in). Russian Museum, Leningrad, USSR

Constructivism

The Constructivists wanted to create a new art for the new society which the Communists were shaping in the USSR. They therefore created a visual vocabulary based on abstract geometric forms which they believed could speak to everyone. They used this vocabulary in paintings, furniture and fashion design, architectural plans and so on. The idea was to take art out of the hands of the privileged few and display it "... *in the streets, in trolley*

A Constructivist-style propaganda train. The slogan is in support of spreading the revolution internationally.

cars, factories, workshops, and the homes of the workers" (Vladimir Mayakovski, 1918). The Constructivists' aims were only partially achieved, however, as after the revolution the Soviet régime turned its back on them.

● Willrich's Family Portrait

You may be wondering what is propagandist about this seemingly innocent image. It is typical of the art promoted by the Nazis between 1933 and 1945. The family represents Hitler's ideal because it is "aryan" (uncorrupted with foreign blood). Yet when you contrast the "purity" of this painting with the persecution by the Nazis of the so-called impure, notably the Jews (see Chagall's White Crucifixion, page 29), the deceitfulness of its message really hits home.

Wolf Willrich: Family Portrait. c1939. Further details unavailable as, like many paintings from the Nazi era, it was later destroyed.

Hitler's battle against modern art

Hitler and the Nazis thought nearly all modern art "degenerate" (degrading and corrupt). They burned thousands of works of art, and forbade **avant-garde** artists to teach or exhibit.

Goebbels (second from right), the Nazi Minister of Propaganda, at the ▶ Degenerate Art Exhibition.

In 1937, the Nazis held a "Degenerate Art Exhibition", to ridicule modern art. It contained works by 112 artists, including Picasso, Ernst and Chagall. They also put on the "Great German Art Exhibition", showing works like Family Portrait (above).

According to Adolf Hitler...
"Art must be the messenger of noble and beautiful things, of all that is natural and healthy."
"And don't talk to me about 'threat to artistic freedom'! ... one does not grant anyone the freedom to use his sordid imagination to kill the soul of a people."
◀ *The Sculptor of Germany*

Other works to look at

• Boris Kustodiev: The Bolshevik. 1920. Tretyakov Gallery, Moscow, USSR

• Diego Rivera: Agrarian Leader Zapata. 1931. MoMA, New York, USA

• Museums such as the Imperial War Museum, London, always exhibit a range of propaganda images.

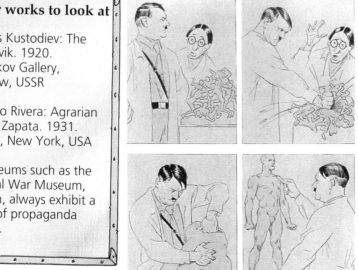

Jugend, 1933 (Garvens)

WAR

Although wars have always caused panic, fear and destruction, most works of art before the 19th century showed only their glorious side. This is because the art was commissioned by ruling powers, such as kings or generals, who used it to celebrate victory, encourage patriotism, and reinforce their power.* These "official" images of war are still produced in the 20th century. However, the more memorable images tend to be the unofficial ones. Because these usually put a more personal point of view, and represent no vested interest, they tend to give a truer, if grimmer, picture of war.

Vorticism

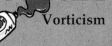

The Vorticists, like the Futurists (see pages 18-19), celebrated the machine age in the years leading up to the First World War. Based in England, their work was more geometric and clearly defined than that of the Futurists. The movement began to break up soon after the war began because it became increasingly difficult for them to see the power of machines as benign.

● Lewis's A Battery Shelled

What do you think this artist felt about the war he is portraying here? There is no sign of blood and guts. Instead, he shows soldiers working hard to clear the debris caused by the shelling of their battery (weapons store) while three officers stand on the sidelines.

Lewis was a gunner in the First World War. When he painted this he was working as an Official War Artist for the British government. The painting was commissioned for a new Hall of Remembrance.

A conflict of styles

Can you detect a contrast in style between the officers in the foreground and the ordinary soldiers and landscape in the background? Before the First World War, Lewis was a member of the Vorticist group (see above). The style of the soldiers reflects the group's interest in drawing people in a mechanical and geometric way. The war affected Lewis's attitude to his art, he said: "*The geometrics which had interested me so exclusively before, I now felt were bleak and empty. They wanted filling.*" This may be one reason why he gave the officers in this painting more character. But why didn't he do the same for the ordinary soldiers?

The final irony

Although it was probably not Lewis's intention, and certainly not the British government's, the painting can be seen as anti-war. Many people see the robot-like figures as a comment on the way war treats soldiers as fighting machines rather than as human beings.

Percy Wyndham Lewis: A Battery Shelled. 1919. Oil on canvas. 152.5 x 317.5cm (5ft x 10ft 4in). Imperial War Museum, London, England

Other works to look at

• Wassily Kandinsky: Cossacks (or Battle) (see page 31). 1910-11. Tate Gallery, London, England

• Stanley Spencer: Travoys Arriving with Wounded at a Dressing Station at Smol, Macedonia. 1919. Imperial War Museum, London, England

• David Alfaro Siqueiros: Echo of a Scream. 1937. MoMA, New York, USA

• Paul Nash: Dead Sea. 1940-1. Tate Gallery, London, England

• Mark Gertler: The Merry-Go-Round (illustrated on page 19). 1916. Tate Gallery, London, England

● Picasso's Guernica

In spite of the violence and confusion in this painting, there is little evidence that it is about war at all, and certainly nothing to tell us when or where it is set. Yet we know that Picasso, a Spaniard, painted it in response to the Nationalist bombing of Guernica (a northern Spanish town) during the Spanish Civil War (see below). Picasso was living in Paris at the time. Four days after the bombing, when photographs such as the one on the right appeared in the French press with news of over 2,000 civilian casualties, Picasso set to work on this painting. He finished it in just two months.

A survivor standing in front of the ruins of Guernica.

Pablo Picasso: Guernica. 1937. Oil on canvas. 349.25 x 776.6cm (11ft 5¹/₂in x 25ft 5³/₄in). Prado Museum, Madrid, Spain

What does it mean?

Scholars have analyzed every detail. All Picasso would say was, "*The horse represents the people, and the bull* brutality and darkness*". The expressions and poses of the people and animals, and their exaggerated, angular shapes, convey their suffering clearly. Why do you think Picasso chose such a sombre colour scheme? Could it have been to reinforce the painting's mood of despair?

The Spanish Civil War

The Spanish Civil War (1936-9) was a power struggle between the right-wing Nationalists, led by General Franco, and the left-wing Republicans. Franco, supported by Nazi Germany and Fascist Italy, eventually won the war.

Guernica's journey to Spain

Picasso didn't want the painting to be shown in Spain until Franco was dead or deposed. First exhibited in Paris in 1937, it then toured to raise money for the Republican cause, ending up at the Museum of Modern Art in New York. Picasso died in 1973, Franco in 1975 and finally, in 1981, Guernica reached the Prado, Spain's national museum.

* **A horse cries in agony as it falls to the ground, with the end of a spear emerging between its legs.**

* **Here, a mother mourns the dead child in her arms.**

* **This soldier lies dismembered on the ground. In one hand he holds a broken sword, from which springs a flower. Could this be a sign of hope?**

* **The light bulb at the centre of the sun may be a statement about the crime against nature that has been committed.**

* **This woman's clothes are on fire. She falls screaming from a burning house.**

* **Here, a woman watches from a window**. In one hand, she holds a lamp. This may represent the Lamp of Truth mentioned in the Bible.**

* **Another woman lunges towards the centre of the picture. Her arms are wide open in a gesture of despair.**

---

* Bulls are present in a lot of Picasso's work; see, for example, page 33. He was fascinated by the ritualized cruelty of bullfights.
** This figure is borrowed from a 17th century **Old Master** painting of the "Massacre of the Innocents", a story in the Bible.

DREAMS

The world of dreams, fantasy and imagination has had greater appeal in some periods than others. The Romantics*, late 19th century Symbolists (such as Gauguin) and the Expressionists all tapped it in their different ways. In 1919, the psychologist Sigmund Freud published a book called The Interpretation of Dreams, in which he claimed that dreams symbolically express our unconscious desires. This work had a great impact on 20th century thought and was a key influence on Surrealist artists in particular.

● Rousseau's The Sleeping Gypsy

What gives this painting its strange, dream-like quality? The gypsy and lion look unnaturally stiff - as if frozen in an instant of time. And there are no footprints in the sand, so how did they get there? Perhaps it is a dream landscape, which only exists in the mind. Rousseau usually paid great attention to detail in his work, so it is unlikely that he would have left out footprints if he had meant this to be a realistic scene.

  What may not have been deliberate, though, is the rather crude, two-dimensional style, which adds to the haunting quality of the work. Rousseau (a customs officer**) taught himself to paint, and tried to imitate the **Old Masters**. Yet the French **avant-garde** of the early 20th century admired his work precisely for its child-like innocence and imaginative power.

Henri Rousseau: The Sleeping Gypsy.
1897. Oil on canvas. 129.5 x 200.6cm
(4ft 3in x 6ft 7in). MoMA, New York, USA

● Surrealism

Founded in Paris in 1924, by the writer André Breton, the Surrealist group developed many of the ideas of the Dada movement (see page 52). The word surreality means beyond or above reality. The Surrealists aimed to link the world of dreams and real life to create an absolute reality, and they used unusual techniques to do this. Ernst, for example, experimented with **frottage**, while Miró starved himself to induce hallucinations. Some Surrealist works are eerie and disturbing, others are very amusing - especially those which bring together unlikely objects. In a famous 3-D work, for example, Dalí put a plastic lobster on top of a real telephone, in such a way that it resembled the receiver.

New Yorker Album, 1937. (Carl Rose © 1937)

A Surrealist family has the neighbours in to tea.

Misunderstood?

Rousseau wanted to give this picture to his native town of Laval. However the townspeople, used to more sophisticated works, ridiculed it. Rousseau became a figure of fun and didn't help matters by making up stories about his artistic methods. For example, he said that his numerous paintings of jungles were inspired by his travels in Mexico. In fact, he only got as far as *Le Jardin des Plantes* (a large botanical garden in Paris). Instead of painting his animals from life, he copied them from an illustrated children's book. Do you consider the technical awkwardness of his paintings a strength or a weakness?

* The Romantic period (late 18th - early 19th century) in European culture was a reaction against the Enlightenment, which preceded it.
** Rousseau's nickname was "Le Douanier", French for customs officer.

● Dalí's The Persistence of Memory

In The Sleeping Gypsy the dream-like quality comes in part from the artist's child-like style. By contrast, here it is Dalí's super-realism, emphasizing the weird subject-matter, which conjures up a nightmarish world. Why should Dalí have made the painting so small (see dimensions below)? Perhaps it was to add to the intensity of the image. Dalí called his works *"hand-painted dream photographs"*.

What does the painting mean? The limp watches may suggest the disintegration of normal time. Insects, feeding on them as if on rotting flesh, reinforce this idea. Yet a Freudian interpretation would surely see the watches as symbolic of sexual impotence.

The caricature of Dalí's own head, with eyes shut, as though dead or asleep, recurs in many of his works.

Strand, June 1946 (John Art Sibley)

Madman or genius?

Dalí is probably the most famous Surrealist artist. This is not just because of his strange and thought-provoking work. He was always trying to shock people, and once said, *"The only difference between me and a madman is that I am not mad!"*. Like many other modern artists*, he was interested in the connection between madness and creativity.

Dalí was only six when he sold his first painting. By the time he was 75, he was so famous that a letter would reach him bearing only the word España (Spain being his native country), and a sketch of his moustache.

Salvador Dalí

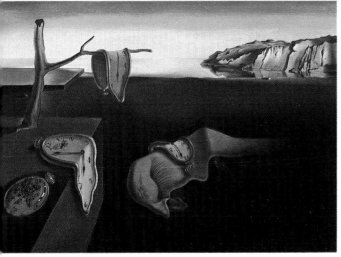

Salvador Dalí: The Persistence of Memory. 1931. Oil on canvas. 24.1 x 33cm (9½ x 13in). MoMA, New York, USA

Other works to look at

• Giorgio de Chirico: The Nostalgia of the Infinite. 1913-14. MoMA, New York, USA

• Marc Chagall: The Poet Reclining. 1915. Tate Gallery, London, England

• René Magritte: The Reckless Sleeper. 1927. Tate Gallery, London, England

• Joan Miró: Painting. 1927. Tate Gallery, London, England

• Meret Oppenheim: Object (Fur Breakfast). 1936. MoMA, New York, USA

● Ernst's Forest and Dove

Perhaps the most striking thing about this painting is the contrast between the light and dark areas and the intricate patterns this creates. But if you look closely, you will see a strange caged bird in the centre of the dark area and, prompted by the title of the work, you may recognize treetops within the patterns. To achieve the bark-like effect, Ernst used a technique called **frottage**, using random rubbings from various surfaces as a basis for imaginative compositions. Many of Ernst's pictures show forests as mysterious and scary. This may recall his childhood when, entering one for the first time, he felt both enchanted and terrified. Like Miró (see page 11), Ernst saw birds and humans as closely linked. So this vulnerable-looking dove may represent the artist himself.

Max Ernst: Forest and Dove. 1927. Oil on canvas. 100.3 x 81.3cm (39 x 32in). Tate Gallery, London, England

* For example van Gogh (see page 8), Munch (see page 12) and Dubuffet (see page 17).

RELIGION

Western art is no longer dominated by images of Christianity, as it once was (see page 4). The main reason for this is that over the past 300 years or so, faith has been gradually undermined by science and rational thought. Many people in the West now look elsewhere for meaning in their lives, often to a non-specific spirituality (see pages 30-31). Artists who *have* tackled traditional Christian themes have sometimes caused offence both by using avant-garde styles, and by seeming to challenge traditional doctrine.

● Nolde's Life of Christ

This painting is one section of Nolde's nine-panelled altarpiece on the life of Christ. Some people considered it blasphemous. Can you imagine why?

The strong colours, lack of detail and crude, even careless-seeming application of the paint make it seem very primitive, compared to the idealism of traditional Nativity paintings. Notice how Christ is painted almost as a physical extension of Mary. Doesn't this emphasize the bond between them? Combined with the foetus-like quality of the baby and the dark, wide-eyed gaze of the parents, this makes the mood of the painting seem unusually intense.

Emil Nolde: Life of Christ: The Nativity. 1911-12. Oil on canvas. 100 x 86cm (39 x 33in). Emil & Ada Nolde Foundation, Seebüll, Germany

A love of the primitive

Nolde, like most other German Expressionists, was a great admirer of tribal art and culture. He even travelled to New Guinea in the South Pacific to experience a "primitive" lifestyle at first-hand.

Here is an example of the kind of primitive art Nolde admired. Considering the similarities between the two works may help you understand what it was that Nolde wanted to imitate.

African sculpture: Mother and child. 20th century. Polished hardwood. Approx. 12.5cm (5in) high. Private collection

Other works to look at

• Paul Gauguin: The Vision after the Sermon (Jacob and the Angel). 1888. Scottish National Gallery of Art, Edinburgh, Scotland

• James Ensor: The Entry of Christ into Brussels. 1889. Musée Royal des Beaux-Arts, Antwerp, Belgium

• Georges Rouault: Christ Mocked by Soldiers. 1932. MoMA, New York, USA

• Graham Sutherland: Deposition of Christ. 1946. Fitzwilliam Museum, Cambridge, England

● Bacon's Three Studies for Figures at the Base of a Crucifixion

The religious themes of Nolde's and Chagall's paintings are instantly recognizable, but what about the one on the right? The title helps explain the tormented expressions on the faces of these writhing, sub-human creatures, but why do you think Bacon left the actual crucifixion out of the painting? Perhaps it would have looked too gruesome. But surely it would be difficult to imagine anything much more gruesome than what actually appears? Like many artists during the Second World War, Bacon found it difficult to believe in the existence of a benevolent God who would come to the rescue of mankind. Could this be why Christ "the saviour" is absent?

Bacon uses the Expressionist devices of exaggeration and distortion to convey extreme emotion in the figures and to suggest fierce heat (perhaps the fires of hell?) in the background to the painting.

Francis Bacon: Three Studies for Figures at the Base of a Crucifixion. c1944. Oil on board. Each 94 x 73.7cm (37 x 29in). Tate Gallery, London, England

Chagall's White Crucifixion

Here, controversially, Chagall shows Jesus as a Jewish martyr. He wears a Jewish prayer shawl as a loin-cloth, and at his feet is a Jewish ceremonial candle-holder. The inscriptions above his head translate as "Jesus of Nazareth, King of the Jews". A man at the lower left of the picture wears a placard which, before the artist painted it out, read "Ich bin Jude" (I am a Jew). Chagall, himself a Russian Jew, did this painting in 1938, to confront Christians with the truth about the Nazi persecution of the Jews, which by this time was well under way.

Marc Chagall: White Crucifixion. 1938. Oil on canvas. 155 x 139.5cm (61 x 55in). The Art Institute of Chicago, Chicago, USA

The storyline

Chagall was brought up in a part of Russia rich in Jewish folklore. This may account for the strong storylines in many of his paintings.

• On the right, a German soldier desecrates, then sets fire to a synagogue.

• On the left a rabble, waving red flags, surges up the hill. Do you think Chagall saw any hope for the Jews in Communism?

• Burning, overturned houses suggest a world turned upside-down.

• Just below the houses, a boatload of refugees tries to escape.

• In the foreground people dressed in the traditional clothes of Eastern European Jews flee scenes of horror.

• At the top, biblical figures look on weeping.

Jews in Nazi Germany were sometimes forced to wear humiliating placards.

Jewish Persecution in 1938

9th June–Munich synagogue destroyed by the Nazis

15th June–1,500 German Jews taken to Nazi concentration camps

10th August–Nuremberg synagogue destroyed by the Nazis

End October–over 15,000 Polish Jews sent back to Poland

November–outbreak of pogroms (organized persecution of the Jews by gangs of thugs)

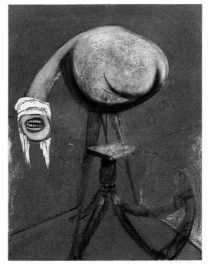

SPIRITUALITY

The decline of organized religion in the West left a gap in people's experience which some artists felt art could fill. The idea that a work of art could meet a spiritual need may seem odd, but in different ways, each of the works shown here aims to do just that.

● **Gauguin's Where do we come from? What are we? Where are we going?**

Paul Gauguin: Where do we come from? What are we? Where are we going?. 1897. Oil on canvas. 139.1 x 374.9cm (54³/₄ x 147¹/₂in). Museum of Fine Arts, Boston, Massachusetts, USA

Other works to look at

• Auguste Rodin: The Cathedral. 1908. Musée Rodin, Paris, France

• Frank Kupka: Amorpha, Fugue in Two Colours. 1912. National Gallery, Prague, Czechoslovakia

• Barnett Newman: Adam. 1951-2. Tate Gallery, London, England

• Mark Tobey: Edge of August. 1953. MoMA, New York, USA

• Cecil Collins: Angel of the Flowing Light. 1968. Tate Gallery, London, England

• Thérèse Oulton: Deposition. 1989. Tate Gallery, London, England

Gauguin said: *"In painting, one must search for suggestion rather than for description, as is done with music."* What does this painting suggest to you? The sizes and spacing of the figures are inconsistent, suggesting that the image should be read on a symbolic, rather than a realistic level.

On the far right is a baby (symbolizing birth?), and on the far left crouches an old woman (symbolizing death?), so perhaps Gauguin meant the figures to represent the stages of human life. The figure picking an apple is probably a reference to Eve, from the Old Testament story of the Fall of Man. The bluish statue to her left was inspired by the ancient Buddhist art of South East Asia (it is known that Gauguin took some photographs of this kind of art with him to the South Seas). These allusions to different religions add weight to the idea that the message of the painting is a spiritual one. Do you think Gauguin meant it to answer the questions posed in the title? and if so, do you think he succeeded in his aim?

An island paradise?

In 1891, Gauguin emigrated from Paris to Tahiti and later to the nearby Marquesas islands. He was attracted to Polynesia because he believed primitive art and life to be superior to so-called civilization. He wrote about his life in Tahiti in a book called Noa Noa. In it he said, *"After the disease of civilization life in this world is a return to health"*. However, Tahiti's native culture had been corrupted since its colonization by the French and, ironically, venereal disease introduced by traders was rife. The Polynesian religion and way of life had all but disappeared.

While Gauguin continued to idealize the South Seas in his art, he became less and less happy with the reality of life there. His disillusionment, combined with the news of the death of his favourite daughter (whom he had abandoned, with the rest of his family, when he emigrated), led him to attempt suicide soon after painting Where do we come from? What are we? Where are we going?

Malevich's White on White

Kasimir Malevich: Suprematist Composition: White on White. 1918. Oil on canvas. 80 x 80cm (31½ x 31½in). MoMA, New York, USA

In contrast to the Gauguin painting (far left) this work gives us almost no clues to its possible meaning. Unless we dismiss it as incomprehensible (as some critics did when it was first exhibited), the only way in which we can respond to it is on an instinctive level. This is precisely what Malevich intended. In 1917, the year of the Russian Revolution, many of his fellow Russians were using their art to promote social change. Yet Malevich's work was becoming more and more mystical. In the catalogue for the exhibition in which this painting appeared, Malevich said, "*I want you to plunge into whiteness... and to swim in this infinity*". What other associations does the colour white have for you?

Does it work?
Now you know that Malevich was trying to encourage spiritual contemplation by painting like this, does it change your view of the work? Bear in mind that this reproduction lacks the size and texture of the original, so you lose a lot of its impact. Consider, too, that though this minimal style of painting is now almost a cliché in modern art, when it was first painted, no one had ever seen anything like it.

Suprematism

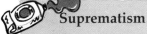

Malevich thought that art should be quite separate from (and superior to) nature, and used geometric forms in his work because they do not exist in nature. He believed that by using them he could achieve "*the supremacy of pure feeling ... in the pictorial arts*" - hence his choice of the term Suprematism to describe his work. This painting was one of a series of abstract works done between 1913 and 1919, inspired by this ideal.

Even Malevich's coffin was adorned with geometric forms

Kandinsky's Cossacks
Although it seems abstract, there is much more in this painting to analyze than in White on White. But perhaps we should be wary of trying too hard to pick things out. Like Gauguin, Kandinsky wanted his art to *suggest* meaning, as music does, rather than stating it plainly.

Even so, there are enough hints to conclude that this is an outdoor scene (a rainbow, centre; hills, left and right; a fortress, with birds flying above it, top right). The title, Cossacks, alerts us to the presence of some soldiers. These could be the red-hatted figures (three in the foreground; two more, mounted on bird-like horses, fight with sabres in the top left-hand corner of the painting).

Wassily Kandinsky: Cossacks (or Battle). 1910-11. Oil on canvas. 94.6 x 130.2cm (37¼ x 51¼in). Tate Gallery, London, England

Is this battle real or symbolic? Kandinsky was interested in mystic philosophies, one of which said that our age of corrupt materialism would end in a cosmic battle, heralding a purer age This may be what Cossacks is really about.

Cossacks* during the First World War

* Cossacks were light horsemen in the Russian army.

31

AN ART OF IDEAS

One of the features which distinguishes modern art from what preceded it is its self-consciousness. Many of the works reproduced in this book exemplify this because, as well as exploring particular themes, they also challenge accepted views about the role of art itself. The artists whose work is shown here go even further. They emphasize the *ideas* behind their works of art, in order to play down their status and potential monetary value as *objects*. Ironically, though, once their approach had lost its shock value, the objects came to fetch high prices on the art market.

● Duchamp's Fountain

You may be wondering how anyone could claim this urinal, laid on its back and ironically entitled Fountain, as art. If you are, you would not be alone in doubting its validity. In 1917, Duchamp, a Frenchman and a prominent member of the Dada group, was appointed to the jury of the First New York Society of Independent Artists. This society was supposedly committed to maintaining a broad-minded attitude towards art. However, when Duchamp submitted his urinal, signed R. Mutt (the name of a firm of toilet manufacturers), his fellow jurors rejected it and hid it behind a partition throughout the exhibition. In response, Duchamp resigned from the jury.

This was not the first time Duchamp had shocked people with his **ready-mades**. He had already exhibited Bicycle Wheel (a bicycle wheel mounted on a kitchen stool) and, even simpler, Bottle Rack, which he had bought in a bazaar.

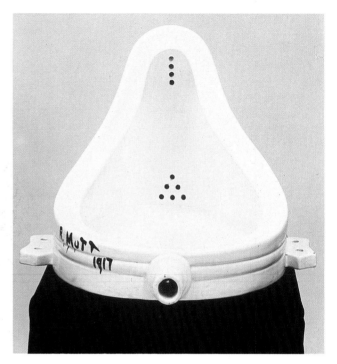

Marcel Duchamp: Fountain. 1917. Ready-made (porcelain urinal turned on its back). 61cm (24in) high. Sidney Janis Gallery, New York, USA

Dada

Dada was a short-lived but important international movement. Sparked off by the horror and absurdity of the First World War, it set out to undermine the social and artistic conventions of middle-class society. Dada may have taken its (deliberately absurd) name from the French childish slang for hobby-horse. The movement was born in 1916 when Hugo Ball and Emmy Hennings opened a club called the Cabaret Voltaire* in a seedy area of Zurich, in neutral Switzerland. They invited artists and poets - the more outrageous the better - to perform and exhibit. The club soon became very popular.

Emmy Hennings and Hugo Ball

In defence of R. Mutt
Duchamp said mischievously of Fountain, *"Whether Mr Mutt has made the fountain with his own hands or not is without importance. He chose it... he created a new thought for this object".*

What was Duchamp's point?
There was an underlying seriousness in Duchamp's actions. He was challenging the idea that artists have to have technical skill and that art objects must be unique. He claimed that objects became works of art just because he chose to display them. In theory, anyone could reproduce one of his ready-mades, and indeed, others have. His variations on the idea included the "reciprocal ready-made" and the "ready-made aided". The former is a work of art that takes on a mundane role (he suggested, for example, using a Rembrandt painting as an ironing board!). The latter is a **found object** altered by the artist, the best-known one being Duchamp's version of the Mona Lisa (1920) which sported a beard and moustache.

* The choice of name was ironic. Voltaire was a famous 18th century rationalist philosopher, yet performances at the club attempted to undermine rationalism.

Picasso's Head of a Bull

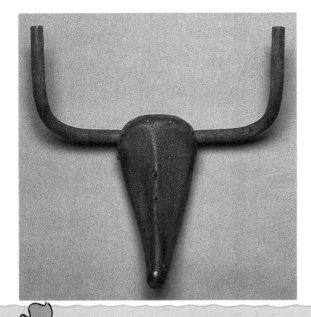

Duchamp might well have chanced upon the same mass-produced objects as Picasso has used here (a leather bicycle saddle and a pair of handlebars). However, he would probably have called them Bicycle Saddle and Handlebars and left it at that. By a leap of the imagination, Picasso has transformed these

Pablo Picasso: Head of a Bull. 1943. Assemblage. 33.5 x 43.5 x 19.5cm (13¼ x 17 x 7½ in). Musée Picasso, Paris, France

mundane objects into an uncannily evocative approximation of a bull's head. Doesn't the result seem to possess the same almost magical quality as the bulls' heads in prehistoric cave paintings?

Although from the date of this work, you might think that Picasso was following in Duchamp's footsteps, he and his friend Georges Braque had in fact begun to work with unconventional materials as early as 1912 (see page 52).

Conceptual Art

Members of this 1970s movement believed that the concept behind a work of art was more important than its physical expression. The purpose of the art object was merely to communicate ideas or record events, in the form of photographs, texts, tapes, videos and so on. The movement grew rapidly, and internationally. Many of the works were deliberately banal, others set out to amuse or to shock (see the examples on the right).

* Vito Acconci described in photos and words how he stepped on and off chairs each day, and compared the different ways in which he did it.

* Iain and Ingrid Baxter of the N.E. Thing Co. wrapped all the contents of a four-room flat in plastic bags, and exhibited them.

* Bruce Nauman photographed himself spitting out a jet of water and called it Self-Portrait of a Fountain (after Duchamp).

Stuart Brisley: And for today ... nothing. 1972

* Stuart Brisley lay for hours at a time in a bath full of filthy black liquid and simulated entrails. This exhibition took place in the dimly-lit bathroom of a London art gallery and lasted for two weeks.

Arnatt's I'm a Real Artist

This man may look like the popular image of an **avant-garde** artist - bearded and vaguely bohemian-looking - but surely an artist isn't an artist just because he says he is? Yet Duchamp could claim that a bottle rack was a work of art, just because he chose to see it that way, so why shouldn't this man proclaim himself an artist in the same way?

Surely Arnatt's intention (like Duchamp's) is to make us question the function and status of artists in our society.

Keith Arnatt: I'm a Real Artist. Photo-piece. 1972. 122 x 122cm (48 x 48in). Oriel Mostyn, Llandudno, Wales

Other works to look at

• Morton Schamberg: God. c1916. Metropolitan Museum of Art, New York, USA

• Piero Manzoni: Line 4.9 metres and Line 18.82 metres. Both 1959. Tate Gallery, London, England

• Bruce McLean: Pose Work for Plinths I. 1971. Tate Gallery, London, England

ART OUTSIDE THE GALLERY

Until the late 18th century, ordinary people had very little access to so-called "high" art (literature, paintings, opera, ballet and so on). Only the very rich owned works of art and the type of art which was accessible to everyone was limited to statues and monuments in public places and religious art in churches. Then, around the turn of the 19th century, the first art galleries and museums were built, with the idea that everyone should be able to look at "important" paintings and sculptures. Yet an increasing number of 20th century artists rejected what they felt to be the exclusivity of public galleries and the commercialism of private ones. Instead, they chose to create works which, by their very nature, were incompatible with the gallery environment.

Art in public places

Public monuments (such as the Royal Artillery Memorial below) have long been an accepted part of our cityscapes. If people objected to them, it was more often for what they represented than for artistic reasons. Modern public sculptures, on the other hand, cause controversy because their only function is to enhance our surroundings and whether they do this can only be a matter of opinion.

Murals

Whereas much modern art tries to communicate important truths to as wide an audience as possible (but may often fail to do so), murals tend to have greater relevance to people living nearby than to outsiders. Murals are often painted by local people (generally under the supervision of a trained "community artist"). Because they are usually painted in a more or less naturalistic style and often take local and/or political issues as themes, they can perhaps claim to bridge the gap between "high" art and the general public. Most murals are temporary fixtures, often painted to cheer up sites which are due for demolition or redevelopment. All this, and their sheer size, makes them unsuitable for display in galleries.

These two murals were painted in 1978 (left) and 1982 (right) on the same wall in Shepherd's Bush, London, England.

C.S. Jagger's Royal Artillery Memorial, 1925, Hyde Park Corner, London, England

Fountain at Château Chinon, France, by Niki de Saint Phalle and Jean Tinguely.

Feminist art

Several groups of contemporary artists have rejected art galleries for political reasons. A common complaint is that they are too commercial and cater for a minority who are "in the know". Feminist artists come into this category and they have sought alternative places to exhibit their work, partly to reach a wider audience, but also because they feel excluded from and misunderstood by what they see as the white, male, middle-class values of the art world. Their work tends to be distinctly different from the mainstream.

Feminist artists often prefer unconventional, usually undervalued media, such as fabric, **found objects**, photography and performance to traditional **fine art** media. Their choice of subject matter is also unusual - often celebrating specifically female areas of experience, not normally dealt with by men (female sexuality and childbirth, for example).

Recently, however, some feminist artists have returned to conventional media and techniques, using them for their own purposes (see Rego, pages 40-41, for example).

Land art

This movement first appeared in the USA in the late 1960s. Most of the work was created in a landscape setting, using whatever materials were to hand. Part of its appeal is that in many cases the artist's work is quickly changed, or obliterated completely by the forces of nature. For example, Robert Smithson built a vast spiral jetty from earth and stones, in the Great Salt Lake, Utah, USA. Deposits of salt and sulphur have completely changed the way it looks.

Some Land artists welcomed such impermanence, because it meant their work could not be owned. This undermined the role of the art market which, some feel, corrupts artistic expression. As Land art is often in wild, out-of-the-way places, it can seldom be seen by the public. Many artists therefore record their activities in words, photographs and so on. Unintentionally, these have taken on the mystique and commercial value of conventional artworks.

A HUNDRED MILE WALK

Day 1 Winter skyline, a north wind

Day 2 The Earth turns effortlessly under my feet

Day 3 Suck icicles from the grass stems

Day 4 As though I had never been born

Day 5 In and out the sound of rivers over familiar stepping stones

Day 6 Corrina, Corrina

Day 7 Flop down on my back with tiredness
Stare up at the sky and watch it recede

Long's A Hundred Mile Walk

Richard Long is one of the most famous and successful Land artists (see left). Much of his work consists of going for long, carefully planned walks in wild and lonely parts of the world, inspired by a nostalgia for unspoiled landscapes. Sometimes he leaves his mark by making small changes to the landscape, such as forming a line of stones. More recently he has brought back **found objects** from his walks and used them to form sculptures in art galleries.

Long's romantic attitude to nature

Richard Long: A Hundred Mile Walk. 1971-2. Map, photo, text. 22 x 50cm (8³/₄ x 20in). Tate Gallery, London, England

seems to have struck a chord with the public, with the result that his work has become very popular. Can you sympathize with his approach?

For A Hundred Mile Walk, Long spent several days walking in a complete circle on Dartmoor, following grid references he had mapped out earlier. He recorded his walk in three ways: a map marked his route, one or two lines of poetic text summed up what he felt each day, and a photograph showed the landscape.

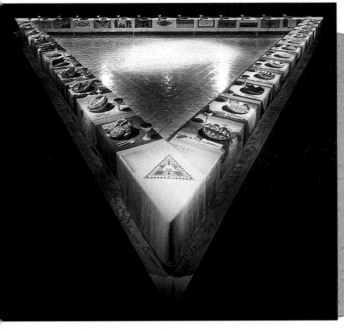

Chicago's The Dinner Party

The Dinner Party is a huge installation which has been exhibited both in art galleries and non-art venues worldwide. It aims to present an alternative view of history, celebrating great women, including artists, writers, political activists - even ancient fertility goddesses.

In a dramatically darkened room, a triangular trestle table (an ironical reference to The Last Supper) is laid with place settings, in the form of embroidered* table mats and ceramic plates, each one dedicated to a particular woman. The plates are decorated with abstract patterns which obviously allude to the female sexual organs. The work is controversial, even among women; but overall, more women than men have sympathized with it.

Judy Chicago: The Dinner Party. 1974-9. Multi-media installation. 14.63 x 14.63 x 14.63m (48 x 48 x 48ft)

---

* Like many feminist artists, Chicago is keen to establish traditionally "feminine" media such as embroidery as a serious means of artistic expression.

ART, ARCHITECTURE AND DESIGN

In recent years, "design" has become a key word. Visual appeal is as important as practicality, whether in a coffee pot or an office block. Less obvious is the extent to which styles in design and architecture are influenced by fine art (painting, sculpture and so on). In some cases, the styles are developed by artists and then taken up by the commercial world (see the Op art fashion on page 19). In others, such as those below, artists became involved in design and worked closely with architects in an attempt to bring together painting, sculpture, architecture and design. The following influential movements shared a desire to use their art to rebuild society after the First World War.

De Stijl

De Stijl (the Style) was founded in Holland in 1917. One of its leading members, Piet Mondrian, is best known for his abstract paintings (see right). Influenced by mystical philosophies, he believed that there are two aspects to human nature - active and passive, male and female, and so on. To express this in his art, he used horizontal and vertical lines. He also used primary colours, because he thought these, too, symbolized the fundamentals of life. Mondrian and his colleagues published a magazine, also called "de Stijl", to spread their ideas. They wanted to combine all the visual arts to create a harmonious living environment.

Piet Mondrian: Composition with Red, Yellow and Blue. 1922. Oil on canvas. 42 x 50.2cm (16¹/₂ x 19³/₄in). Stedelijk Museum, Amsterdam, Holland

De Stijl in 3-D

Other members of De Stijl shared Mondrian's ideas and translated them into three dimensions. The examples below are by the architect Gerrit Rietveld. The Schröder house still stands in Utrecht, Holland.

◄ **Schröder house, 1924. Notice its simple vertical and horizontal lines and primary colours.**

**Red, yellow and blue chair, ►
1917-19. Although the back and seat tilt (which might have displeased Mondrian, see right) they meet at a right angle.**

Was Mondrian a fanatic?

Mondrian believed in the superiority of the horizontal and vertical to such an extent that when other members of De Stijl introduced diagonal lines into their work (see below), Mondrian left the movement in disgust. Perhaps it is surprising, then, that in his private life Mondrian enjoyed informal, expressive hobbies such as jazz and dancing.

Interior of the Café d'Aubette Cinema Dance Hall, 1926-8, by Theo van Doesburg.

● Constructivism

As with De Stijl and the Bauhaus (see right), the theories of this Russian movement (see page 23) applied not just to painting and sculpture but also to designs for clothes, furniture and buildings. Unfortunately, the harsh economic conditions in Russia at the time of the Revolution meant that many of the more ambitious projects could not be carried out.

Constructivist design for sportswear by Varvara Stepanova. Gouache on paper. 28.5 x 21.8cm (11¼ x 8½in). 1923.

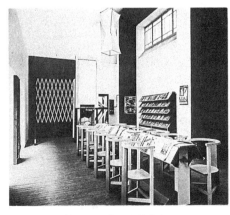

Design for a Workers' Club by Alexander Rodchenko. Exhibited in Paris in 1925, but never actually built.

* Many Bauhaus (and De Stijl) designs are still in production today.

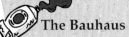

The Bauhaus

The Bauhaus (House of Building) was an influential art school founded by the architect Walter Gropius in Germany in 1919. Many famous painters, such as Kandinsky (see page 31), taught there. Like members of De Stijl, Gropius and his colleagues wanted to combine all the arts to create a better environment. This was reflected in the range of different arts disciplines which were taught. Students had the chance to work with a much wider selection of techniques and materials than was usual in such institutions. In 1933, the Bauhaus was closed by the Nazis, who thought its **avant-garde** ideas and teaching methods morally corrupting.

The Bauhaus look

The Bauhaus aimed to achieve just the right balance between style and function. Mass-production meant that their unadorned, geometric designs became available to ordinary people*.

The Bauhaus building in Dessau. Designed by Walter Gropius, it was completed in 1926. It is celebrated for the simplicity of its design.

Marcel Breuer's first tubular steel chair with fabric seat, back and arm rest, 1925. ▶

Globe lamp by Wilhelm Wagenfeld, 1923-4. The metal base conceals the electrical wiring.

Other works to look at

● Maurice Novarina (architect): Notre-Dame-de-Toute-Grâce. 1937-49. Assy, Haute-Savoie, France. Contains works by Léger, Chagall, Lipchitz and other artists.

● Henri Matisse: Chapelle du Rosaire. 1948-51. Vence, France

● Basil Spence (architect): Coventry Cathedral. c1954-62. Coventry, Warwickshire, England. Contains works by Piper, Sutherland, et al.

MODERN ART AND POPULAR CULTURE

In the past, people had less time and money for leisure pursuits; but pastimes such as song, dance and local crafts flourished in the home and the community. "High" culture (art, opera, ballet, books) was mainly for the rich and privileged. After society became industrialized in the 19th century, mass production and new inventions gradually made a vast array of goods available to many more people and shorter working hours gave people more free time to enjoy them. This is how the popular culture we know today - from paperbacks to pop music, fast food to soap opera - started to evolve.

● Modern art against snobbery

Many people still think that art is for the privileged few, rather than for everybody. Printing has made works of art more widely available through posters, postcards and so on, but cannot truly be said to have popularized them. Buying original works of art is beyond most people's pockets, but visiting an art gallery costs little, so why do so few people go? Some modern artists have asked this question indirectly in their works. When Duchamp pioneered **ready-mades** (see page 32), one of the things he was challenging was the idea that art was produced for an élite (those "in the know"). Later, Pop artists tried to do something similar. Instead of using real objects, as Duchamp did, they used images from popular culture as the inspiration for paintings, screen prints, sculptures and so on.

Pop art

The brash consumer culture which developed in the USA and Europe during the 1950s was in marked contrast to the austerity of the preceding war years. In the late 50s and early 60s, it inspired a modern art movement in England and America, known as "Pop art". Pop artists took images from cartoons, advertising, the cinema - even the fast food industry. They enlarged them, repeated them or distorted them, to comment, sometimes satirically, on the use of the original images in western society.

● Lichtenstein's Whaam!

On the face of it, this painting looks just like two frames from a 1960s strip cartoon. All the usual things are there - the speech bubble, the Batman-style exclamation, the action, the bright, flat colour. You can't tell here, but one of the main differences between this painting and a real cartoon is its size - Whaam! is the length of a small room. What do you think this suggests about Lichtenstein's attitude to his subject matter? Perhaps he is suggesting that strip cartoons are worthy of our serious attention. On the other hand, by inflating the size of his "super-heroes", he may be using irony to diminish them in our eyes. Doesn't this exaggeration, combined with the blandness of line and flatness of texture, neutralize the shock-effect of its violent subject matter? Lichtenstein said, *"One of the things a cartoon does is to express violent emotion in a completely mechanical and removed style"*.

Roy Lichtenstein: Whaam!. 1963. Acrylic on canvas. 172.7 x 406.4cm (68in x 13ft 4in). Tate Gallery, London, England

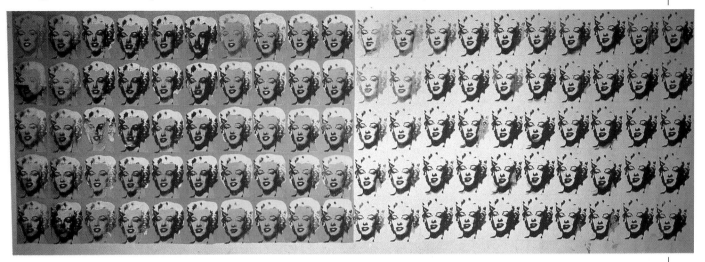

This is one of many paintings of Marilyn Monroe that Warhol produced in the early 1960s, immediately after her controversial death*. Although Warhol claimed that his works had no deep significance beyond their surface appeal, the Marilyn pictures all make use of a screen-print based on a publicity photograph of Monroe.

The fact that Warhol preferred an impersonal printing process to painting by hand, has been seen in itself as a comment on the way the star's screen image was unconnected with her real self. Doesn't the repetition of the image add to the de-personalizing effect? Notice how Warhol has blurred her image and

Andy Warhol: Marilyn x 100. 1962. Acrylic and silkscreen on canvas. 205 x 567.7cm (6ft 8in x 18ft). Saatchi Collection, London, England

changed from colour in the left-hand panel to black and white in the right-hand one. Was this a reminder of Marilyn's fate or a comment on mortality in general?

Marilyn Monroe before she was "made-over" by the film industry. ▶

Other works to look at

- Peter Blake: Got a Girl. 1960-1. Whitworth Art Gallery, University of Manchester, Manchester, England

- Claes Oldenburg: Floorburger. 1962. Art Gallery of Ontario, Toronto, Canada

- James Rosenquist: Marilyn Monroe, I. 1962. MoMA, New York, USA

- Richard Hamilton: I'm Dreaming of a White Christmas. 1967-8. Kunstmuseum, Basel, Switzerland

Modern art in everyday life

Pop art shows the influence of popular culture on modern art, but the movement of ideas was not just one-way. There are many examples of modern (and "traditional") art cropping up in everyday life. The Bauhaus (see page 37) consciously blurred the boundaries between art and everyday objects such as chairs and light fittings. Since then there have been many examples of references to modern art in popular culture, from Picasso-inspired tee-shirts to the advertisements shown here. Some advertisements can be seen as tributes to the artists they imitate, others poke fun at **avant-garde** art, exploiting the popular suspicion of it.

This television advertisement for beauty ▶ products uses figures from Gauguin's paintings (see page 30) to conjure up an idealized image of the South Seas.

▲ **This advertisement for washing powder was part of a campaign featuring witty imitations of work by several famous modern artists.**

39

* No one is sure whether she died by accident or suicide. Some even suspect foul play.

RECENT TRENDS

The Conceptual and Minimal art of the 1960s and early 70s had largely dealt with the role of art itself. By the 1980s both artists and public had tired of this and there was a gradual return to art which related more obviously to the real world. Traditional materials and figurative subject-matter* became fashionable again - a trend which made art more saleable.

Trends in the 1980s

• Many artists started using styles and techniques from the past, while at the same time questioning their relevance to the present. Baselitz's painting (below right) is one example.

• Some artists carried on the **avant-garde** tradition of using unorthodox materials, often to make a social or political point. See the works here by Tony Cragg and Nam June Paik.

• More and more female artists made their mark. But instead of rejecting traditional techniques and media as symbols of male power (see page 34), many feminists now began to use them for their own purposes. Paula Rego's work (far right) is a case in point.

• By the end of the 80s, American artists had come to the fore again. During the 80s they had been overshadowed by European artists (particularly German and Italian ones). Jeff Koons's sculpture, shown here, is typical of the witty, rather brash work they were producing.

• By the beginning of the 1990s, **figurative art** was still prominent. However, lately there is evidence of a partial return to a rather cooler, more detached approach in both abstract and figurative art.

● Cragg's Britain seen from the North

Tony Cragg: Britain seen from the North. 1981. Mixed media. 369.6 x 698.6cm (12ft 1½in x 22ft 1in) and 170.2 x 59.4cm (67 x 23in). Tate Gallery, London, England

This work consists of many fragments of mass-produced objects (such as plastic plates) which Cragg collected from London streets and waste-sites and stuck straight on to the gallery wall. Why do you think he used these particular materials? It could be a comment on modern consumerism and its harmful effect on our environment. And why has he turned the map of Britain on its side and added the figure (for which, incidentally, he drew around his own body)? Most of Britain's power and wealth are concentrated in London and the South, so perhaps it is Cragg's way of showing what life looks like to the "have-nots".

● Baselitz's Adieu

Baselitz is a member of the Neo-Expressionist (literally New-Expressionist) trend. These artists were reacting against the unemotional art of the 60s and 70s by using bold colours and disturbing images. Baselitz's technique and choice of subject-matter clearly owe much to German Expressionist art**. This style usually has a lot of emotional impact. Why do you think Baselitz has painted his subjects upside-down? Some have claimed it is just a gimmick, whereas others see it as a deliberate ploy to introduce a degree of detachment.

Georg Baselitz: Adieu. 1982. Oil on canvas. 250.9 x 298.4cm (8ft 2³/₈in x 9ft 9½in). Tate Gallery, London, England

* The return to figurative art meant that previously neglected artists, such as Golub (see page 21), were suddenly "discovered".
** See, for example, Nolde's Life of Christ: The Nativity on page 28.

Koons's Rabbit

Jeff Koons: Rabbit. 1986. Cast stainless steel. 104 x 48.3 x 30.5cm (41 x 19 x 12in). Saatchi Collection, London, England

In most of his work, Koons uses banal, everyday objects, acknowledging his debt both to the pioneer of **ready-mades**, Marcel Duchamp (see page 32), and to Pop art (see pages 38-39). A novelty balloon like this is just the sort of thing Koons might use in his work, so perhaps this stainless steel replica is a kind of "in-joke". Many people find the sculpture amusing, but quite how profound its message is is another matter. Do you think it is meant to do anything more than make us smile?

Rego's The Maids

How would you like to have these maids waiting on you? They look rather menacing don't they? The title of the painting is taken from a play by the 20th century French writer Jean Genet, but Rego wants us to imagine the plot for ourselves. Some people consider Rego a feminist artist because her main characters are always women and, in her recent work especially, they are usually up to mischief - often (though not always) aimed at men.

Paula Rego: The Maids. 1987. Acrylic on paper stuck on canvas. 213.4 x 243.9cm (7ft x 8ft). Saatchi Collection, London, England

Other works to look at

- Sandro Chia: The Idleness of Sisyphus. 1981. MoMA, New York, USA

- Stephen McKenna: Venus and Adonis. 1981. Tate Gallery, London, England

- Ken Currie: Glasgow Triptych. 1986. Scottish National Gallery of Modern Art, Edinburgh, Scotland

- Sonia Boyce: From Tarzan to Rambo. 1987. Tate Gallery (print room), London, England

Paik's Fin de Siècle II

Video art has existed since the 1960s, and Nam June Paik, a Korean artist, was one of its pioneers. It is only recently, though, that video art has stopped being regarded as a poor relation in the art world. Fin de Siècle II (End of the Century II) is a huge video installation made up of over 200 television sets stacked against a museum wall (only part of it is shown here). Controlled by hidden computers, the images and soundtrack coming from the sets include David Bowie, a man and a woman dancing, a skeletal character who resembles the comedian Max Headroom, and many other barely recognizable but eye-catching fragments. It seems likely that the overall lack of story or message is intentional. All the work conveys is the overwhelming nature of modern communications technology and perhaps this is Paik's point.

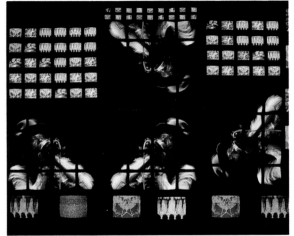

Nam June Paik: Fin de Siècle II. 1989. Variable dimensions. Whitney Museum of American Art, New York, USA

AT WHAT PRICE?

One of the things which makes people most puzzled and sceptical about modern art is the staggeringly high prices it sometimes fetches. Quality in a work of art has never been a matter only of the apparent technical skill of the artist. However, the modern emphasis on imagination and originality (subjective qualities which are extremely difficult to put a price to) quite often makes the commercial value of a work seem arbitrary. Below you can find out how the price of a work of art is, in fact, determined.

● Who sets the price?

It is very rare for a modern artist to sell a work of art directly to a customer. Works usually sell through dealers or at auction.

Art dealers

Dealers take at least one third of the selling price of a work. This is how they cover their costs (rental of gallery space, publicity and so on) and make a living. The higher the price they get for a work, the more money their share represents, so they charge as much as they can.

Auctions

Experts at an auction house estimate the selling price of an artwork before a sale. However, auctions are notoriously unpredictable. On 15 May 1990, a little-known work by van Gogh called Portrait of Dr Gachet was put up for auction at Christie's, New York (see right). Many people thought that the depression in the art market would prevent it from fetching the price which the experts had predicted. Imagine their surprise when the painting sold for $82,500,000 - double the predicted price.

● How do they set the price?

Dealers and auction house experts base a work's commercial value on the following factors:

• The artist's reputation. This depends on how many exhibitions his or her work has been included in, particularly solo exhibitions. It also depends on whether the artist has been noticed by art critics who often put exhibitions together themselves, as well as writing critiques of other exhibitions. Later on, the artist's works may have been bought by museums or well-known private collectors, and books may have been written about him or her.

● Who buys the "masterpieces"?

Sadly, not all works of art are bought purely for love. Although most collectors are initially motivated by an interest in art, very valuable works are sometimes bought as status symbols or for investment. Prices are often beyond the reach of state-funded museums, and only rich individuals or corporations can

• Fashion. Changes in fashion can lead to the "discovery" of an artist after they have been ignored for years, or even after their death.

• The size of the work, cost of materials used and time taken to produce it (usually only factors when the artist is starting out).

• The rarity value of the work. If the artist is dead, the price of his or her works tends to increase.

• The price the artist's work has fetched before, allowing for inflation.

• The state of the art market.

I don't know much about art but I know what appreciates...

18 Oct. 1969 (Steinberg © 1969)

afford them. For example, Portrait of Dr Gachet was bought by a Japanese paper manufacturer.

The rewards of success

Some artists, such as van Gogh, could barely make ends meet when they were alive. This makes the high prices their works fetch today seem ironic. Others made a fortune. When Picasso died in 1973 his estate was worth millions (see right).

Works of Art
1,876 paintings, rugs, and illustrated books
7,089 drawings
149 sketchbooks
18,095 etchings
3,181 linocuts
6,112 lithographs
1,355 sculptures
2,880 ceramic works

Value: 1,251,663,200 Ffr

Real Estate
Farm "Notre-Dame-die-Vie," Mougins
Villa "La Californie" Cannes
Chateau at Vauvenargues
Chateau at Boigeloup

Value: 10,000,000 Ffr

In his will, Picasso bequeathed 39 paintings and 14 drawings by other artists, such as Matisse, to the French government. On top of this, his heirs gave 800 of Picasso's own works to the government instead of inheritance tax.

Just a load of old bricks?

In 1972, the Tate Gallery, London, bought this sculpture for several thousand pounds*. The purchase provoked a storm of controversy. Andre's use of actual bricks (which are dismantled when the work is in storage) follows in the footsteps of many modern artists, above all Marcel Duchamp (see page 32). However, unlike Duchamp who was mocking traditional values, Andre's aim was to reveal the beauty in humble, man-made objects arranged in a precise mathematical order. The Tate Gallery argued that as Britain's major public gallery showing modern art, it should buy works which reflected important historical trends; in this case

Minimalism (see page 54). But the public objected to the high price paid for a work which they thought lacked artistic value.

Carl Andre: Equivalent VIII. 1966. Fire bricks. 12.8 x 68.6 x 229cm (5in x 27in x 7ft 6¹/₈in). Tate Gallery, London, England

The role of the critic

There is nearly always a connection between the artistic "worth" of a work of art (as judged by critics and the general public) and its commercial value (see "How do they set the price?" above left). But just as the price is fixed by assessing a range of factors which coincide at a particular point in time, so critics are influenced in their opinions by their background, education and experience - and times change. You only have to remember how the critics received the French Impressionists (see page 8) to realize that, at worst, they often just reflect society's prejudices.

So if you read exhibition reviews and books about the history of art, try to read as widely as you can, and bear in mind that there is no "absolute" truth when it comes to judging a work of art. Your opinion may be as valid as anyone else's.

What happens at an auction?

The auction-house sends out a catalogue in advance, giving details of the works of art which will be on sale and an estimate of the sums they will fetch. The works can also be seen at a preview.

On the day of the auction, each bidder is registered and given a numbered bidding paddle, to avoid confusion. Then, when an item comes up for sale, would-be buyers signal that they want to enter or raise the bidding by holding up their paddle.

Van Gogh's Portrait of Dr Gachet being auctioned at Christie's, New York, on 15 May 1990.

People who are unable to attend the auction can bid by telephone or by registering an absentee bid. In both cases a representative bids on their behalf until the work reaches the maximum price the

client is willing to pay.

When no one wants to bid anymore, the auctioneer closes the bidding by hitting his hammer on the auction table. The item is sold to the person who made the last bid.

The top five

Here are the five most expensive works of art sold at auction (up to August 1991)

1. Portrait of Dr Gachet (van Gogh): $82,500,000.
15 May, 1990

2. Au Moulin de la Galette (Renoir): $78,100,000.
17 May, 1990

3. Les Noces de Pierrette (Picasso): FFr 300,000,000.
29 November, 1989

4. Irises (van Gogh): $53,900,000.
11 November, 1987

5. Self-Portrait: Yo Picasso (Picasso): $47,850,000.
9 May, 1989

*The gallery never revealed the exact sum, and various figures were quoted in the press.

THE ROAD TO FAME?

The myth of the dedicated artist, starving in a garret, but remaining true to his art, to some extent, still persists. Most contemporary artists care too much about their artistic integrity to measure success or failure purely in financial terms. Some may even be prepared to sacrifice the possibility of a more lucrative career for the fulfilment of doing something they enjoy. However, failure to make enough money at their art may mean having to abandon it as a career. Whether it is your ambition to become an artist yourself, or you are simply curious about the modern-day art scene, you can find out here about the harsh realities of life for today's aspiring young artists.

● Starting off in the art world

You might think that originality and confidence are more important qualifications for a would-be artist than conventional artistic skill. At first glance, few of the works in this book show much evidence of the latter. However, with a few notable exceptions (Rousseau, for example) most modern artists *have* had some kind of technical training.

● Going to art college

Art college courses vary greatly in their approach to teaching. Some are quite unstructured, whilst more traditional ones allocate specific times to skills such as life drawing. Consider which type is likely to suit you best before you apply.

Good art colleges are not easy to get into. Most degree course tutors select students on the basis of their academic qualifications and their recent work. If called for interview, take your portfolio along (substituting colour slides for large pieces or sculptures) and be ready to explain why and how you did each piece.

At the end of your course, your work will be exhibited in an end-of-year show. These are sometimes visited by art dealers and museum curators looking for new talent.

● Keeping in touch with the trends

The first modern artists stuck together (both geographically and intellectually). They often lived in close-knit groups in a particular city, and so could share studios and meet for discussions in cafés. One example of a thriving artistic community was Paris in the 1910s and 20s.

Café La Coupole, Paris. A popular meeting place for artists in the early part of the century. ▶

Today attention tends to focus on several artistic centres at once, rather than just one. As an individual artist, it may seem daunting to try to keep abreast of what's going on, but modern communications have made it much easier than it was in the past. Here are some ways of keeping in touch:

• Visit museums and galleries regularly, at home and abroad.

• Read the art critics in newspapers and magazines.

• Read art magazines. These range from glossy, lavishly illustrated ones which discuss issues in contemporary art to cheaper ones which may be practical or theoretical in approach. There are some books and magazines recommended on pages 60-61.

• Talk to other artists, course tutors, exhibition organisers and dealers, whenever possible. Contacts will not only keep you abreast of developments, but can be the key to survival for today's artists.

Earning a living

Many celebrated artists have found it hard to make ends meet early on in their careers. With a few well-known exceptions (van Gogh being perhaps the most famous one) most went on to find recognition within their own life-time. Picasso's life-story is the kind of rags-to-riches tale which gives hope to many an unknown artist. In 1904, he was sharing a draughty and primitive studio complex with 30 other artists. But by his death, he was a multi-millionaire and probably the most celebrated modern artist ever.

The Paris studio complex known as the Bateau Lavoir, where Picasso became a leading member of the avant-garde.

The role of the art dealer

In the past, patrons and collectors were the most influential people in the art market. They commissioned works of art and therefore had a say in the type of work that was produced. Gertrude Stein (see right), for example, helped launch the careers of Picasso, Braque and Matisse.

From the 19th century on, however, art dealers gradually started to take over from patrons and collectors as the driving force behind the art market. Art dealers are middle-men who sell uncommissioned work directly to the general

Gertrude Stein, art patron and collector.

public. Finding an art dealer is the key to commercial success for an artist. In return for promoting his or her work in the dealer's own gallery

and, wherever possible, in museum shows, the dealer takes commission (usually at least a third of the selling price of the artist's work).

Degree shows apart, it can be very difficult these days for an unknown artist to attract the attention of a dealer. The best way to approach one is through a contact. An influential art critic, or an artist who is already represented by the dealer, might be prepared to introduce you, if they think your work is good enough. Otherwise your chances of being noticed are slim. However, there are other options (see right).

Promoting yourself

Although gaining access to art dealers, and thereby to commercial galleries, is difficult for an unknown artist, it is still possible to show your work in publicly-funded galleries and exhibition spaces. Their organisers are often pleased to look at unsolicited work.

Visit as many galleries and exhibitions as you can and make a short list of those likely to take an interest in your type of work. Then send them examples of your work, in the form of 35mm colour slides, with details of the dimensions and media of the original works and any other relevant information.

New Yorker, 8 June 1968 (Koren)

However, for every success story there must be dozens of artists (perhaps some potential "greats") who have endured a life-time of hardship in obscurity. Whether they were never recognized because their work was out of sympathy with the prevailing fashion or because they lacked talent, would be impossible to say. It may be tempting to change your style to suit the current trend, but this is no guarantee of commercial success and may well limit any real artistic progress in your work.

Most people see art as a vocation rather than a career. This is mainly because of the enduring myth

about the artist's lifestyle, mentioned in the introduction. There may indeed be some truth in the idea that artists need to be exceptionally dedicated to succeed, because of the uncertain nature of the art market. Even so, it can be useful, on one level, to judge an artistic career in strictly practical terms. Ask yourself "Can I make a living at it?" and "Do I find it fulfilling?". If the answer to both these questions is "Yes!", then it is surely as valid a career choice as any other. However, even relatively successful artists sometimes have to supplement their income by working in other areas occasionally.

• Adding another string to your bow

It may be worth cultivating a secondary artistic skill, such as graphic design or book illustration, which would allow you to take on freelance work from time to time. Alternatively, a temporary job which is completely unrelated to the art world may prove less of a distraction from your artistic career.

• Residencies and teaching posts

Artists who are prepared to combine their own artistic activities with a commitment to education or communication, may be suited to a career as an art teacher or artist-in-residence. Artists-in-residence are usually employed for a fixed period by galleries, arts centres and sometimes by institutions such as factories and prisons. In exchange for studio space and living expenses, the artist must be available at certain times to demonstrate and explain his or her work to visitors to the studio.

• Business sense

On one level, working as an artist is like running a small business. It helps to have a basic understanding of accounting. You also need to be sufficiently business-minded to charge realistic prices, deliver commissioned work on time and maintain a level of output which keeps you in profit.

ABOUT THE ARTISTS

● **ANDRE, Carl**
Born 1935
American Minimal sculptor
Since 1966, Andre has made sculptures out of mass-produced objects (such as bricks) laid horizontally on the ground. The sculptures are dismantled when they are not on display.

● **ARNATT, Keith**
Born 1930
British Conceptual artist
Since the late 1960s, his work has questioned the role of art and the artist in western society, often in a humorous way.

● **BACON, Francis**
Born 1910
British painter
Born in Dublin, Ireland, Bacon moved to London in 1925, working as a decorator. He started painting pictures in his late teens, without any formal training. Between 1934 and 1944 he virtually stopped, discouraged by a lack of interest in his work. He caught the public eye in 1944 with Three Studies for Figures at the Base of a Crucifixion (see page 29) and has since been hailed as one of the most important living British artists.

● **BALLA, Giacomo**
1871-1958
Italian painter
Between about 1900 and 1910 the style of Balla's work was influenced by Pointillism. After 1910, he became involved with the Futurist group. From then on all his work conveyed the idea of speed and movement, although by 1912 he was depicting it in a more abstract way.

● **BASELITZ, Georg**
Born 1938
German painter and sculptor
He was born Georg Kern in Deutsch-Baselitz in East Germany. After moving to West Berlin in 1957, he changed his surname to that of his birthplace in homage to Emil Nolde, who had done the same (see page 50). Baselitz first studied in East, then West Berlin. Although he held his first one-man exhibition in West Berlin in 1963, his work only really attracted attention in the early 1980s.

● **BLUME, Peter**
Born 1906
American painter
Blume was born in Russia, but emigrated to the USA in 1911. He trained at the Art Students' League in New York, and spent some time in Italy in 1932 and 1936. In the 1930s, he became known for pictures combining meticulous detail with surreal imagery. His most famous works are The Eternal City (see page 20) and South of Scranton (1931, Metropolitan Museum of Art, New York).

● **BRAQUE, Georges**
1882-1963
French painter
Braque initially worked as a housepainter, following in his father's footsteps. Then, from 1902-4 he studied art in Paris. In 1906, he became associated with the Fauve painters, then from 1907-14 he worked closely with Picasso. Together they pioneered Cubism, and in 1912 Braque became the first modern artist to introduce collage into his work. Unlike Picasso, he remained more or less true to Cubist principles for the rest of his career.

● **BREUER, Marcel**
1902-81
Hungarian architect and designer
Breuer moved to Vienna in 1920, intending to become a painter and sculptor, but soon left to study at the Weimar Bauhaus. At only 22, he became director of the furniture department there. He pioneered mass-produced furniture using bent steel tubes as frames. He left the Bauhaus in 1928 to be an architect and interior designer in Berlin. He later lived in London and the USA.

● **CÉZANNE, Paul**
1839-1906
French painter
Born in Aix-en-Provence, Cézanne initially studied law, but abandoned this to become an artist in 1861. He moved to Paris and soon became associated with the Impressionists. In 1870 he returned to Aix-en-Provence and lived there for the rest of his life.
In the 1860s, Cézanne's work was rather dark in colour and often violent and/or brooding in subject-matter. His work of the 1870s was Impressionist in style and subject-matter. From the 1880s on, he increasingly stressed an almost geometrical structure in his paintings, and a sense of harmony, thereby earning the description of Post-Impressionist. The work of this last period had a crucial influence on Cubism.

● **CHAGALL, Marc**
1887-1985
Russian-French painter
Chagall was born into a Jewish family in Vitebsk, western Russia. He studied art in St Petersburg (now Leningrad) from 1907-10, and in Paris from 1910-14, where his unusual imagination soon attracted the attention of the **avant-garde**. In 1914, he moved back to Russia, but left for France again in 1923 and, apart from a few years spent in the USA (1941-8), lived there for the rest of his life. Nearly all his work is concerned with the Russian-Jewish world of his childhood.

● **CHICAGO, Judy**
Born 1939
American feminist artist
She changed her surname to that of her birthplace as a gesture of rebellion against a society that gives priority to the father's name. In the 1960s, Chicago's work was mostly abstract and not obviously feminist. However, since the early 1970s she has worked, often with other women,

on unconventional, multi-media projects addressing subjects such as female sexuality and creativity.

● CRAGG, Tony
Born 1949
British sculptor
Part of a new "wave" of British sculptors that came to prominence in the early 1980s, Cragg was born in Liverpool, England. He studied at Gloucestershire College of Art, then at Wimbledon School of Art and the Royal College of Art, both in London. His first one-man exhibition was in London in 1979. He now lives and works in Germany.

● DALÍ, Salvador
1904-89
Spanish painter
Dalí studied in Madrid before becoming an important figure in the Paris-based Surrealist movement in 1929. He was expelled from the group in the late 1930s because of his extreme right-wing political views and blatant self-promotion. His work is highly realistic in style and contains often shocking dream-like imagery.

● de KOONING, Willem
Born 1904
American painter
De Kooning was born in Rotterdam, Holland. He studied art in Amsterdam, while at the same time working as a decorator. He emigrated to the USA in 1926.
His early work was traditional. Then in the 1920s-30s, he tried out several different styles simultaneously, influenced by Kandinsky and the late Cubism of Picasso. From the late 1940s onwards, he became a key member of the Abstract Expressionist group, although he also produced **figurative** images at the same time (see page 10).

● DELAUNAY, Robert
1885-1941
French painter
Delaunay trained as a decorator before turning to fine art in 1904. From 1906 onwards, his work reflected his interest in the colour theories of Neo-Impressionism, and from 1910, the year he married fellow painter Sonia Terk, he became involved with the Cubist movement.
Between 1912 and 1913, Delaunay produced a series of almost abstract images which are among the earliest known abstract paintings. They formed the basis for a movement known as Orphism. His work of the 1920s onwards concentrates on urban subjects.

● DOESBURG, Theo van
1883-1931
Dutch painter and architect
Van Doesburg's early work was influenced by Post-Impressionism, then in 1915 he met Mondrian and turned to geometric abstraction. In 1917, he became an organizer and promoter of De Stijl (see page 55). Then in about 1924, he abandoned strict De Stijl principles by introducing diagonal lines into his work.

● DUBUFFET, Jean
1901-85
French painter
Although Dubuffet showed an early talent for art, he did not become a full-time painter until 1942. His work reflects his admiration for graffiti, and the art of children, the untrained and the insane (which he termed "art brut" or "raw art").

● DUCHAMP, Marcel
1887-1976
French painter and sculptor
Possibly the most subversive and influential of all 20th century artists. Duchamp came from a family of painters. He first attracted attention in 1913 with his Nude Descending a Staircase (Philadelphia Museum of Art). He became obsessed with the connection between human bodies and machines: see especially his Large Glass (1915-23, reconstruction in the Tate, London). In 1913 Duchamp created his first **ready-mades** (see page 32).
Despite his successful career, by 1923 Duchamp had virtually abandoned art to become a professional chess player.

● ERNST, Max
1891-1976
German-French painter
Ernst studied philosophy at Bonn University from 1908-14. In 1911 he made contact with the Blaue Reiter group, and eight years later became the leader of the Cologne Dada group. In 1922, he settled in Paris, where he soon became an important member of the Surrealist group. The style of Ernst's work is very varied, and is characterized by his technical inventiveness - for his pioneering experiments with frottage for example, see page 27.

● GAUGUIN, Paul
1848-1903
French painter
Born in Paris, Gauguin spent four years in Peru as a child, before returning to France. His early career as an artist was unconventional, including spells as a merchant seaman and a stockbroker. In the mid-1870s, Gauguin started painting, first in a realist style, and then in an Impressionist one; his work from about 1888 onwards is usually described as Post-Impressionist.
In 1883, he gave up stockbroking to become a full-time painter. He left his wife and family and worked in Brittany from 1886-90, apart from trips to Panama and Martinique and a disastrous two months spent with van Gogh in Arles in 1888 (see page 48). Between 1891 and 1893, then from 1895 until his death, Gauguin lived and worked in the South Seas (see page 30).

GERTLER, Mark
1891-1939
British painter

Gertler's parents were Polish-Jewish immigrants, living in London. He trained at the Slade School of Art in London from 1908-12. His early work shows Jewish figures from the East End of London, from which he was gradually distancing himself. The work he did in the 1920s is mostly of still lifes and nudes inspired by classical sculpture. Gertler committed suicide in 1939 (see page 19).

GIACOMETTI, Alberto
1901-66
Swiss sculptor and painter

Giacometti's father and uncle were both painters, and he himself began his career by studying painting in Geneva from 1919-20. His earliest sculptures were influenced by Cubism, then in the late 1920s and early 30s, Giacometti became involved with the Surrealist group. From the late 1940s onwards, he created the elongated, emaciated figures for which he is best known.

GOGH, Vincent van
1853-90
Dutch painter

Van Gogh decided to become an artist in 1880, after an unsuccessful spell working as a lay preacher. He studied briefly at the Antwerp Academy from 1885-6, before moving to Paris where, under the influence of the Impressionists, the colour and mood of his work lightened. In 1888 he moved to Arles in the South of France. Gauguin visited him there that year and violent disagreements between them provoked van Gogh's first mental seizure. His subsequent emphasis on expressing his emotional state in his work was to earn him the title of Post-Impressionist. In 1890 he moved north to Auvers-sur-Oise where he committed suicide.

GOLUB, Leon
Born 1922
American painter

Golub was born in Chicago, and studied art history at the University of Chicago from 1940-42. He then studied art at the School of the Art Institute of Chicago from 1946-50. His first solo exhibition was held in Chicago in 1950. He married the feminist artist, Nancy Spero, in 1951. His work, which is figurative and dedicated to exposing human cruelty, has only recently received critical acclaim.

GROPIUS, Walter
1883-1969
German architect

Gropius studied at the Colleges of Technology of Berlin (1903-5) and Munich (1905-7), then worked for the pioneering architect Peter Behrens for three years. He started his own practice in 1910. In 1911, he designed the Fagus factory at Alfeld with Adolf Meyer. This steel and glass construction is now considered one of the earliest examples of truly modern architecture. He was director of the Bauhaus from 1919-28, moved to England in 1934, where he practised in partnership with the British architect Maxwell Fry,and finally settled in the USA in 1937.

GROSZ, George
1893-1959
German draughtsman and painter

Grosz studied art in Dresden and Berlin. His satirical tendencies were strengthened by his traumatic experiences in the First World War. He was a committed Communist, and became a leading member of the Berlin Dada group between 1918 and 1920. He is best known for attacking the German régime of the 20s and early 30s. When Hitler came to power in 1933, Grosz fled to the USA.

KAHLO, Frida
1910-54
Mexican painter

Kahlo first began to paint when she was bedridden by a terrible car accident; she had no formal training. Her life was plagued by ill-health and complicated by a turbulent relationship with fellow painter Diego Rivera (see page 15). The style of her work was influenced by Mexican folk art and nearly all her subject-matter was autobiographical. She was hailed by the Surrealists as a kindred spirit, but never joined their group.

KANDINSKY, Wassily
1866-1944
Russian painter

Born in Moscow, Kandinsky studied law, economics and politics at Moscow University, and in 1893 became a university lecturer in law. However, four years later, at the age of 31, he went to Munich to study painting, and soon became active in the artistic **avant-garde** there.

In 1911, he became a founder member of the Blaue Reiter group, then in 1914, he went back to Russia. From 1921-33 he taught at the Bauhaus, during which time his paintings became more geometric. After that he moved to Paris and lived there for the rest of his life.

LEHMBRUCK, Wilhelm
1881-1919
German sculptor

Lehmbruck studied at the School of Applied Art in Düsseldorf from 1895-9, then at the Academy of Art, Düsseldorf from 1901-7. His early work was more or less realistic, then in 1911 he developed his own personal style: elongated forms which are slightly melancholy in mood. He was hailed by many of his contemporaries as the major Expressionist sculptor, although Fallen Man (see page 13) was extremely controversial. In 1919, severely depressed by the First World War, he committed suicide in Berlin.

LEWIS, Percy Wyndham
1882-1957
British painter and novelist

Lewis studied at London's Slade School of Art from 1898-1901, then travelled to Munich, Holland, Spain and Paris. On his return to England in 1901, he became a founder of the Camden Town group (who were influenced by Post-Impressionism). In 1914, he became leader of the Vorticists. His work after the First World War was more realistic than that done pre-war (see page 24).

LICHTENSTEIN, Roy
Born 1923
American painter

From 1939-40, Lichtenstein studied at the Art Students' League in New York, then at Ohio State University from 1940-3. He worked as a commercial artist and freelance designer between 1951 and 1957. His early paintings were Abstract Expressionist in style. From 1957 onwards, he became one of the most popular Pop artists.

LISSITZKY, El (Eliezer Markowich)
1890-1947
Russian painter and graphic artist

Between 1909 and 1919, Lissitzky studied engineering. Between 1916 and 1919 he became a member of a group of Jewish artists (including Chagall) whose aim was to create a national Jewish art in Russia. By 1919, though, he had met Malevich, and transferred his allegiances to Constructivism. In 1922, he left Russia for Berlin, but returned six years later and worked mainly in industrial design and typography.

LONG, Richard
Born 1945
British artist

Long studied at the West of England School of Art from 1963-6, then at St Martin's School of Art, London from 1966-8, specializing in sculpture. Since 1967, all his work has centred on walks he has done in remote areas of the world. He has recorded his experiences in photographs, texts and maps. More recently, he has created sculptures or wall drawings in gallery settings with materials taken from the natural world, such as slate and mud. His type of work is a form both of Land art and Conceptual art.

MALEVICH, Kasimir
1878-1935
Russian painter

Malevich's early work was influenced by Impressionism and Post-Impressionism. Then from 1908-11, his work was more "primitive" in style. In the three years after this, he developed a style called "Cubo-Futurism". However, he is probably most famous for pioneering Suprematist art from around 1913 to the late 1920s. After this he returned to **figurative** work.

MATISSE, Henri
1869-1954
French painter and sculptor

Matisse studied law, but abandoned it to become an artist in 1891. He studied at the Académie Julian, and the École des Beaux-Arts, both in Paris. His early work was quite dark and realistic. Then, in around 1905, he became leader of the Fauve group, and his work became much brighter in colour, and expressed his belief in the pursuit of pleasure. In 1948, he began work on paper cut-outs (see page 9), and from 1948-51, decorated the inside of the Chapelle du Rosaire in Vence, France.

MIRÓ, Joan
1893-1983
Spanish painter

Miró studied art in Barcelona. His earliest work was influenced by Fauvism. In 1919, he paid his first visit to Paris, and was briefly influenced by the Cubist works he saw there. By the early 1920s, he was in contact with a number of Surrealists in Paris, and actually joined the movement in 1925. From 1924 onwards, his work was inspired by primitive art, the art of children, and above all, his belief in the power of the imagination and the unconscious mind.

MONDRIAN, Piet
1872-1944
Dutch painter

Mondrian studied at the Amsterdam Academy. His early landscape paintings were realistic. In 1908, he started using lighter colours, and went through a Symbolist phase. In 1911 he went to Paris and started developing Cubist ideas in an abstract way. He returned to Holland in 1914, co-founded De Stijl with van Doesburg, then moved to Paris again in 1919. By the early 1920s, he had developed the radical abstract style for which he is best known.

In 1940 Mondrian moved to New York, where he died. His New York paintings are more dynamic and expressive of city life than any of his earlier work.

MONET, Claude
1840-1926
French painter

Monet was born in Paris, though he grew up in Le Havre. He studied art in Paris, where he met a number of other future Impressionists. In the 1870s he was very poor, but by the 1880s, he started becoming more financially successful. He moved to Giverny and began to paint in series, for example, Rouen Cathedral, haystacks and waterlilies.

MOOR, Dimitri (Dimitri Orlov)
1883-1946
Russian graphic artist

Moor is one of the best-known of the more traditional artists who put their art completely at the service of the Russian Revolution of 1917. His work, which was very influential, was recognized in a Soviet government order of 1922.

MOORE, Henry
1898-1986
British sculptor

Moore studied at the Leeds School of Art, Yorkshire and the Royal College of Art, London. From about 1930 onwards, he became one of the most important and influential figures in British art and by the 1940s had achieved international recognition. His favourite subject was the female figure although, inspired by primitive art and his love of landscape, he totally disregarded anatomical accuracy. He was a pioneer of the "truth to materials" approach, which allowed the stone, metal or whatever, an active role in the making of the sculpture.

MUNCH, Edvard
1863-1944
Norwegian painter and graphic artist

Munch studied in Oslo, then travelled extensively in France, Italy and Germany. In 1908 he suffered a serious mental illness and lived in Norway from then on. His work of the 1890s was realistic in style, but brooding in mood. By the 1890s, his work was more Symbolist, and had an important influence on German Expressionism.

In 1892 an exhibition of his work in Berlin was closed down because it was considered shocking. From 1908 onwards, his work became less personal, but he returned to a more emotional approach in the 1920s.

NOLDE, Emil (Emil Hansen)
1867-1956
German painter

Nolde changed his name from Hansen to that of his birthplace in about 1904. He studied art in Flensburg and Karlsruhe, then worked in St Gall, Munich, Paris and Copenhagen before settling in Berlin in 1906. For the next two years, he was associated with the Die Brücke group, and became one of the most powerful German Expressionist painters. In 1941, he was denounced as "degenerate" by the Nazis (despite having been a member of the Nazi party). They forbade him to paint, but he continued to do so in secret.

O'KEEFFE, Georgia
1887-1986
American painter

O'Keeffe studied art in Chicago and New York, then taught in Texas and Virginia until 1918. She then gave up teaching to become a full-time painter. In 1916 she met Alfred Stieglitz, a photographer and modern art dealer who recognized and encouraged her talent, and in 1924 they married. In 1929 she "discovered" the New Mexican desert, and went to live there in 1946, after Stieglitz's death. She is known chiefly for her dramatically abstracted landscapes, her paintings of flowers and other natural forms, and also for her resolutely independent lifestyle.

PAIK, Nam June
Born 1932
Korean video artist

Paik was born in Seoul, North Korea, and studied music and art history in Japan and Germany. In the early 1960s he began, through association with an anarchic group called Fluxus, to challenge the conventions of "high art". He began working with video in 1965 and has since incorporated music, video images and TV sets in sculptures and installations.

PICASSO, Pablo
1881-1973
Spanish painter, sculptor and graphic artist

Picasso was born in Malaga, Spain, the son of a painter. He is probably the most famous of all modern artists, due not only to his critical and financial success, but also to his personal charisma and colourful private life. He was an extremely precocious student. Between 1900 and 1904, he divided his time between Paris and Barcelona, finally settling in Paris in 1904. 1901-4 was his "blue period", when his paintings were sombre in mood. This was followed by his "rose period" when his work was more serene. Between 1907 and 1914, he formed a close friendship with Braque, and together they pioneered Cubism. Much of his work of the 1920s to mid 1930s was influenced by Surrealism. After the Second World War, Picasso settled in the South of France. He died in 1973 and was given a state funeral.

POLLOCK, Jackson
1912-56
American painter

Born in Wyoming, Pollock studied at the Art Students' League, New York in 1929. During the 1930s, he worked in a style influenced by American Regionalists (a group of painters in the 30s and early 40s who celebrated American rural and provincial, rather than city life), Mexican muralists and Surrealism. He became famous for the drip paintings he did from 1947; he literally dripped paint from a stick, brush or even the paint tin, on to the horizontal canvas. By the early 1950s, however, he started reintroducing recognizable imagery into his paintings. In 1956, he was killed in a car crash, though many people believe this was suicide, as he was known to be suffering from drinking problems and depression.

REGO, Paula
Born 1935
Portuguese-British painter

Rego was born in Lisbon, Portugal but she studied art at the Slade, London, from 1952-6. She settled permanently in London in 1976. Often described as a feminist artist, Rego's work is **figurative**, and she uses traditional materials. Her subversiveness very often stems from the storyline of her paintings which frequently depict rather sinister-looking female characters.

RIETVELD, Gerrit
1888-1964
Dutch architect and designer

Rietveld worked as an apprentice in his father's joinery workshop from 1899-1906, then studied architecture from 1911-15, running his own cabinet-making business at the same time. He was a member of the De Stijl group from 1918-31, and his work as an architect and furniture designer reflects the group's principles of functional geometric units and primary colours.

RILEY, Bridget
Born 1931
British painter

Riley was born in London, and studied at Goldsmith's College, London, from 1949-53, and at the Royal College of Art, London from 1952-5. She is best known for her ingenious Op art work which dates from the early 1960s onwards. Initially, she did these paintings in black and white, but from 1965 introduced colour into them.

RODCHENKO, Aleksandr
1891-1956
Russian painter, designer and photographer

Born in St Petersburg (now Leningrad), Rodchenko studied at the Kazan Art School from 1910-14, then at the Stroganov Art School in Moscow. In about 1915, he started producing geometric abstract works. From 1918 onwards, he became extremely active in the new art organizations set up in the wake of the Russian Revolution, and applied Constructivist principles to paintings, furniture, clothes, photographs, stage design and typography. In the mid-1930s, however, he returned to easel painting.

ROUSSEAU, Henri ("le douanier")
1844-1910
French painter

Rousseau was the son of a tinsmith, and had very little formal education. After a career in the Army, he worked in the Customs and Excise department ("le douanier" means customs officer). In 1885, he retired and set up as an amateur painter, doing portraits and other commissions. In 1886, he was introduced to the Parisian art world, and started exhibiting there regularly. Between about 1906 and 1914, he was hailed by the Parisian **avant-garde** as having great natural talent, and was appreciated for the very naïvety that he sought to overcome.

SEURAT, Georges
1859-91
French painter

Seurat studied at the École des Beaux-Arts in Paris. To begin with he produced only black and white drawings, moving into colour later.

Seurat's subject matter was influenced by the French Impressionists, although his technique of colour mixing (known as Divisionism or Pointillism) was much more scientific than theirs, and certain aspects of his paintings refer to the classical tradition. Seurat died of meningitis, aged only 31, but his ideas were taken further by Paul Signac and a group of younger artists who became known as the Neo-Impressionists.

STEPANOVA, Varvara
1894-1958
Russian painter and designer

Stepanova studied at the Kazan Art School, where she met Alexander Rodchenko, her future husband. She moved to Moscow in 1912, and attended the Stroganov Art school there. She became active in revolutionary art organizations from 1918 onwards. Until 1921, she concentrated on Constructivist easel painting and graphics; thereafter on textile design.

WAGENFELD, Wilhelm
Born 1900
German industrial designer

Wagenfeld was born in Bremen. He studied at the State drawing academy at Hanau and, after qualifying as a silversmith, went to the Weimar Bauhaus, where he became an instructor. After leaving the Bauhaus, his designs became less rigorously "pure" and he went on to teach at the the Berliner Kunsthochschule, and then to work in industry, designing glassware, metalwork and plastics.

WARHOL, Andy
1930-87
American painter and film-maker

Warhol was born in Pennsylvania to Czech immigrant parents. He studied art in Pittsburgh from 1945-9, then worked as a commercial artist for advertising agencies in New York. By the early 1960s, Warhol was the most famous and controversial of all Pop artists. Nearly all of his best-known work involves the repetition, by means of silk-screen printing, of images taken from the world of commerce, advertising and the media (see page 39).

WILLRICH, Wolf
Dates unknown
German painter

Studied at Dresden Art Academy after a traumatic experience as a soldier in the First World War. He was well known during the Nazi era both for his images of "pure" Nordic types and for his battle against "degenerate" art. In 1937, the same year as the notorious "Degenerate Art Exhibition", Willrich published a book entitled "The Purification of the Temple of German Art".

MOVEMENTS

Below is a summary of some of the major modern art movements. Many of them are also discussed elsewhere in the book; when this is the case, the relevant page number has been given. You will see that many of the artists' names are in capital letters. This means that you can find one or more of their works reproduced in this book.

Name, dates and place of origin	Leading members	Main characteristics
Abstract Expressionism Late 1940s-late 50s USA (see also pages 5 and 10)	Gorky, de KOONING, Motherwell, Newman, Rothko, Tobey, POLLOCK	Artists produced large-scale, dramatic abstract paintings. There were two main types: "Action Painting" (see page 5), and the quieter "Colour-field Painting" which used broad expanses of colour and relied more on colour association. This movement was largely responsible for New York displacing Paris as the centre of the art world after the Second World War.
Bauhaus 1919-33 Germany, first Weimar, then Dessau, then Berlin (see also page 37)	BREUER, Feininger, GROPIUS, KANDINSKY, Klee, Moholy-Nagy, van der Rohe, Schlemmer	An influential German art school which was eventually closed down by the Nazis. Each student studied art, architecture and design with the ultimate aim of creating a better living environment for everyone. Its design principles were based on admiration for geometry and the machine.
Conceptual art Late 1960s-70s Mainly USA, GB and Italy* (see also page 33)	ARNATT, Burgin, Craig-Martin, Dibbets, Haacke, Kelly, Kosuth, LONG, Manzoni, McLean, Weiner	Conceptual artists emphasized the ideas underlying works of art, often as a protest against the commercialism of the art world. They often used photos, text, etc. to document an action or event, or to express ideas.
Constructivism c1917-early 20s Russia (see also page 23)	Exter, LISSITZKY, Popova, RODCHENKO, STEPANOVA, Tatlin	A geometric abstract art movement. Artists were initially influenced by Suprematism, but after the Russian Revolution they tried to help create a new society by applying geometric design principles to all areas of life (architecture, furniture, clothes design, etc.).
Cubism c1907-early 20s Paris (see also page 6)	BRAQUE, DELAUNAY, Gris, Laurens, Léger, Lipchitz, PICASSO	A style pioneered by PICASSO and BRAQUE which drew attention to the contradictions involved in depicting a 3-D scene on a 2-D surface. Analytical Cubism (1907-12) broke down real objects into different parts. Synthetic Cubism (1912-14) built up recognizable images from abstract parts using ready-made materials such as newspaper.
Dada c1914-20 International but particularly Zurich, Berlin, Cologne, Hanover, Paris, Barcelona and New York (see also page 32)	Arp, Ball, DUCHAMP, ERNST, Picabia	A movement of irreverent, unbridled protest against the state of western society that led to the First World War. Members saw art as decadent and middle class. They staged events (now often called "Happenings") designed to shock, and created works out of unconventional materials, or based on chance.

* In Italy, Conceptual art was also known as Arte Povera.

Movement	Artists	Description
Expressionism **1905-early 20s** **Germany and Austria** **(see also page 12)**	Heckel, Jawlensky, KANDINSKY, Kirchner, Kokoschka, Kollwitz, Marc, Meidner, NOLDE, Schiele, Schmidt-Rottluff	The artists' main purpose was to express emotions and/or a sense of deeper reality, through vigorous brushstrokes, and distortion or exaggeration of shapes and colours. There were two main groups: Die Brücke (The Bridge) and Der Blaue Reiter (The Blue Rider). Van GOGH and MUNCH were key influences*.
Fauvism **c1905-10** **France**	Derain, van Dongen, Dufy, MATISSE, Vlaminck	A group of young painters centred around MATISSE whose work was characterised by strong colour and powerful brush strokes. When they exhibited together in the 1905 Salon d'Automne in Paris, they were named "fauves" (wild beasts), and caused great controversy. Unlike the German Expressionists, their work tended to be joyful.
Futurism **1909-14** **Northern Italy** **(see also page 18)**	BALLA, Boccioni, Carrà, Severini	This movement was founded by the poet Marinetti. Its members rejected the past and instead celebrated the dynamism of the machine age and city life. They published aggressive manifestos and, like the Dada artists, staged "Happenings" designed to shock. Their paintings were initially influenced by Pointillism, then by Cubism, but put greater emphasis than the latter on a sense of movement.
Impressionism **c1874-86** **France** **(see also pages 8-9)**	Cassatt, Degas, MONET, Morisot, Pissarro, Renoir	The first major **avant-garde** movement. The name was invented in 1874 by a hostile critic, inspired by a painting by Monet entitled Impression: Sun Rise. The Impressionists' aim was to capture the passing moment, by means of a sketchy technique, strong colour and a commitment to outdoor, on-the-spot (**plein-air**) painting, with as little reworking in the studio as possible.
Kinetic art **1960s** **International**	Bury, Calder, Lijn, TINGUELY	Sculpture that actually moves, often using modern technology (such as electricity) to achieve this. It contrasts with Op art which just appears to move. Although artists like Moholy-Nagy had experimented with this idea as early as the 1920s, it did not emerge as a widespread tendency until the 1960s.
Land art **1960s-80s** **Mainly USA and GB** **(see also page 35)**	Christo, Fulton, Goldsworthy, LONG, Oppenheim, Smithson	Art that involves the artist going out into nature (normally in a remote area), and making his or her mark on it. The only record that remains is photographic, sometimes combined with maps, text and so on. More recently, some Land artists have exhibited sculptures made from natural **found objects** inside galleries.

* However, the term Expressionism is sometimes also used to refer to French Fauvism, and to a characteristic of much modern art.

Minimalism Late 1960s-70s Mainly USA (see also page 43)	ANDRE, Judd, Morris	An intellectual sort of art which seems to consist of very little, so that the viewer is forced to scrutinize the formal properties of what is actually there very carefully. The work is usually rigorously geometric and involves the repetition of identical objects. MALEVICH was among the pioneers of this kind of art.
Neo-Expressionism Late 1970s-80s International (but particularly Germany and Italy) (see also page 40)	BASELITZ, Chia, Cucchi, Kiefer, Penck, Schnabel	Widespread and much-publicised characteristic of 1980s art. The work appears to pay homage to earlier 20th century Expressionism (see page 53).
Op art Late 1950s-60s International* (see also page 19)	Agam, Albers, Anuskiewicz, RILEY, Soto, Vasarely	The name is short for Optical art. It refers to a geometric abstract art that manipulates the viewer's visual response and creates the illusion of movement. Artists use theories from the psychology of perception to achieve this effect.
Orphism 1912-13 France	DELAUNAY, Delaunay-Terk, Kupka	A colourful and almost abstract strand of Cubism. It can be seen as one of the earliest attempts to create an abstract art.
Performance art (includes "Happenings") 1960s-present International	ARNATT, Brisley, Gilbert and George, Horn, McLean, Nitsch	This art is related to theatrical performance, but usually has no plot or sense of drama. It is often used to make a political point, exploit the idea of endurance and/or boredom, or simply to entertain. Exists afterwards in the form of photographs.
Pointillism Mid 1880s-90s Mainly France (see also page 15)	Cross, SEURAT, Signac	The technique of applying small, regular dabs of unmixed colour on to the picture surface, relying on scientific theories (such as the precise combination of complementary colours - red/green, orange/blue, yellow/violet). Pioneered by SEURAT, who used the term "Divisionism".
Pop art Late 1950s-60s Mainly USA and GB (see also page 38)	Blake, Hamilton, Hockney, LICHTENSTEIN, Oldenburg, Rosenquist, WARHOL	The apparent celebration of western consumerism after the austerity and rationing of the war years. The artists' work evokes the brash, colourful world of advertising, comic strips and popular entertainment.
Post Impressionism 1880s-90s Mainly France	CÉZANNE, GAUGUIN, SEURAT, van GOGH	A blanket term referring to art that both learnt from and rejected certain Impressionist principles. CÉZANNE and SEURAT tried to regain a sense of order; GAUGUIN attempted to express a world of imagination and spirituality; van GOGH, elemental emotions.

* The French Op art movement was known as Cinétisme or Art Cinétique.

Socialist Realism **1930s-50s** **USSR and other countries in the Communist Bloc** (see also page 22)	Brodsky, Deineka, MOOR	Art promoted by the Stalinist régime in Russia as a propaganda tool. The artists used a realistic, but often melodramatic style to present an idealized vision of Soviet society and its leaders. The movement began to oust Constructivist ideals in the early 1920s, and became a rigid doctrine in the early 30s. Artists had to tow the party line or risk being unable to exhibit or buy materials. Although from the 1950s onwards there was an increasing amount of "unofficial" art produced, Socialist Realism continued to dominate Russian and Eastern European art until relatively recently.
De Stijl **1917-early 30s** **Holland** (see also page 36)	Van Doesburg, van der Leck, MONDRIAN, Oud, RIETVELD, Vantongerloo	A movement founded by van Doesburg and MONDRIAN to promote their use of geometric abstract shapes and primary colours, based on the idea of universal harmony. Their ideas extended to architecture and design as well as paintings. They published a magazine with the same name.
Suprematism **c1913-early 20s** **Russia** (see also page 31)	MALEVICH	MALEVICH expressed the ideas behind this movement in his book "The Non-Objective World". He wrote of his wish to create a vocabulary of geometric abstract shapes entirely independent of the visible world, and expressing pure artistic feeling. Although by 1917-18 his aims became more mystical, he greatly influenced the Constructivist artists.
Surrealism **1924-40s** **Mainly Paris** (see also page 26)	CHAGALL, de Chirico, DALÍ, ERNST, Klee, Masson, Matta, MIRÓ	A movement that drew on certain ideas of Dada, and on the writings of Freud to create an art which was intended to free the viewer as well as the artist by exploring the world of the unconscious and subconscious mind. Some artists used unorthodox techniques such as frottage (see page 27) to do this.
Symbolism **1890s** **International (although mainly France)**	GAUGUIN, Moreau, MUNCH, Puvis de Chavannes, Redon	A literary and artistic movement which, partly in reaction to Realism and Impressionism, emphasized the world of the imagination, of ideas, dreams and emotions. In some respects, Symbolism was a predecessor of both Expressionism and Surrealism.
Vorticism **c1910-14** **England**	Bomberg, LEWIS, Roberts, Wadsworth	A group of London-based **avant-garde** artists inspired by Cubism and Futurism. They rejected the gentility of the English art world and celebrated the excitement and beauty of the machine age. They published a magazine called "Blast". Not surprisingly, the movement did not survive the brutality of the First World War.

MUSEUMS AND GALLERIES

Below is a list of some of the major museums and galleries throughout the world which have comprehensive modern art collections.

National and local holidays vary, so telephone the museum in advance to ensure you don't find it closed when you arrive.

● Australia
Australian National Gallery
Parkes Place, Parkes, Canberra, ACT 2600
Tel. 62 71 2411
Hours: Mon-Sat 10am-5pm, Sun noon-5pm. Closed Good Friday and Christmas Day.

● Austria
Museum Moderner Kunst
consists of two museums:
Palais Liechtenstein, Vienna 9, Furstengasse 1
Tel. 1 34 12 89
Hours: daily 10am-6pm. Closed Tues and national holidays.

Museum des 20. Jahrhunderts, Vienna 3, Schweizergarten
Tel. 1 78 25 50
Hours: daily 10am-6pm. Closed Wed and national holidays.

Osterreichische Galerie des 19. und 20.Jahrhunderts
Oberes Belvedere, Vienna 3, Prinz Eugen Strasse 27
Tel. 1 78 41 14 or 1 78 41 21
Hours: daily 10am-4pm. Closed Mon, Jan 1, May 1, Nov 2 and Dec 25.

● Belgium
Koninklijk Museum voor Schone Kunsten
Leopold de Waelplein, 2000 Antwerp
Tel. 3 238 7809
Hours: daily 10am-5pm. Closed Mon.

Musée d'Art Moderne
1-2 Place Royale, 1000 Brussels
Tel. 2 513 9630
Hours: 10am-1pm, 2-5pm daily. Closed Mon.

● Canada
National Gallery of Canada
380 Sussex Drive, Box 427, Station A, Ottawa, Ontario K1N 9N4
Tel. 613 990 1985 or 990 1980
Hours: from May 1-Sept 3, Sat-Tues 10am-6pm, Wed-Fri 10am-8pm. From Sept 4-April 30, Tues-Sun 10am-5pm, Thurs 10am-8pm. Closed Mon and national holidays.

Art Gallery of Ontario
317 Dundas Street W, Toronto, Ontario M5T 1G4
Tel. 416 977 0414
Hours: Tues, Thurs, Fri, Sat and Sun 11am-5.30pm, Wed 11am-9pm. Closed Mon.

● Denmark
Louisiana Museum of Modern Art
Gl. Strandvej 13, 3050 Humlebaek
Tel. 318 6322020
Hours: daily 10am-5pm, Wed 10am-10pm.

● France
Musée Picasso
Chateau Grimaldi, 06600 Antibes
Tel. 93 34 91 91
Hours: daily 10am-noon, 3-6pm or 7pm, though closes at 5pm from mid-Sept to March. Closed Nov and Tues.

Centre National d'Art Contemporain
Villa Arson, 20 ave Stephen Liegeard 06000 Nice
Tel. 93 84 40 04
Hours: daily 2-9pm.

Musée de l'Annonciade
Place Georges Grammont, 83990 St. Tropez
Tel. 94 97 04
Hours: daily except Tues, June-Sept, 10am-noon, 3-7pm (to 6pm rest of the year). Closed Nov.

Fondation Maeght
06570 St-Paul-de-Vence
Tel. 93 32 81 63
Hours: daily 10am-12.30pm, 2.30-6pm (3-7pm in July and Aug).

Chapelle du Rosaire
Avenue Matisse, 06014 Vence
Tel. 93 58 03 26
Hours: Tues and Thurs only, 10-11.30am, 2.30-5.30pm.

Musée Claude Monet (Académie des Beaux-Arts)
Giverny, 27620 Gasny
Tel. 16 32 51 28 21
Hours: from 1 April-31 Oct 10am-noon, 2-6pm. Gardens 10am-6pm. Closed Mon.

Musée d'Art Moderne de la Ville de Paris
11 ave du President Wilson, 75016 Paris
Tel. 47 23 61 27
Hours: daily 10am-5.40pm, but open until 8.30pm Wed. Closed Mon.

Musée National d'Art Moderne
Centre National d'Art et de Culture Georges Pompidou, 75004 Paris
Tel. 42 77 12 33
Hours: noon-10pm weekdays, 10am-10pm weekends and national holidays. Closed Tues.

Musée d'Orsay
1 rue de Bellechasse, 75007 Paris
Tel. 40 49 48 14
Hours: daily 10am-6pm, but open on Thurs until 9.45pm, and on Sun from 9am-6pm. Closed Mon.

Musée Picasso
Hôtel Salé, 5 rue de Thorigny, 75003 Paris
Tel. 42 71 25 21
Hours: Wed 9.45am-10pm, Thurs-Mon 9.45am-5.15pm. Closed Tues.

Musée de l'Orangerie des Tuileries
Place de la Concorde, Paris
Tel. 42 97 48 16
Hours: daily 9.45am-5.15pm.

● Germany
Altes Museum
Bodestrasse 1-3, 0-1020 Berlin
Tel. 2 03 0381
Hours: Tues-Sat 10am-6pm. Closed Sun and Mon.

Bauhaus-Archiv
Klingelhoferstrasse 14, 1000 Berlin 30
Tel. 30 261 1618
Hours: daily 11am-5pm. Closed
Tues and national holidays.

Brücke-Museum
Bussardsteig 9, 1000 Berlin 33
Tel. 30 831 2029
Hours: daily 11am-5pm. Closed
Tues and national holidays.

Nationalgalerie
Potsdamer Strasse 50, 1000 Berlin 30
Tel. 30 266 2662
Hours: Tues-Sun 9am-5pm. Closed
Mon and national holidays.

Museum Ludwig
An der Rechtsschule, 5000 Cologne 1
Tel. 221 221 2379
Hours: daily 10am-5pm, but open
until 8pm on Tues and Thurs.
Closed national holidays.

**Kunstsammlung
Nordrhein-Westfalen**
Grabbeplatz 5, 4000 Düsseldorf
Tel. 211 133961 64
Hours: daily 10am-5pm, but open
until 8pm on Wed. Closed Mon and
national holidays.

**Wilhelm-Lehmbruck
Museum**
Friedrich-Wilhelm Strasse 40, 4100
Duisberg
Tel. 203 283 2630
Hours: Tues 11am-8pm, Wed-Sun
11am-5pm. Closed Mon and
national holidays.

Museum Folkwang
Bismarckstr. 64/66, 4300 Essen
Tel. 201 181 8484
Hours: Tues-Sun 10am-6pm. Closed
Mon and national holidays.

Neue Pinakothek
Barer Strasse 29, 8000 Munich 40
Tel. 89 238 05195
Hours: Wed-Sun, 9am-4.30pm,
Tues 9am-9pm. Closed Mon and
national holidays.

**Stadtische Galerie im
Lenbachhaus**
Luisenstr. 33, 8000 Munich
Tel. 89 521041
Hours: Tues-Sun 10am-6pm. Closed
Mon and national holidays.

Nolde-Stiftung
Seebüll 2268 Neukirchen
Tel. 4664 364
Hours: March-Nov daily 10am-6pm.
Closed for rest of year and national
holidays.

● Great Britain

Fitzwilliam Museum
Trumpington Street, Cambridge
CB2 1RB
Tel. 0223 332900
Hours: 10am-5pm Tues-Sat and
summer national holidays, 2.15-
5pm Sun. Closed Mon.

National Museum of Wales
Cathays Park, Cardiff CF1 3NP
Tel. 0222 397951
Hours: 10am-5pm Tues-Sat, 2.30-
5pm Sun.

**Scottish National Gallery of
Modern Art**
Belford Road, Edinburgh EH4 3DR
Tel. 031 556 8921
Hours: Mon-Sat 10am-5pm, Sun 2-
5pm.

Imperial War Museum
Lambeth Road, London SE1 6HZ
Tel. 071 735 8922
Hours: daily 10am-6pm. Closed Dec
24-26, Jan 1.

Tate Gallery
Millbank, London SW1P 4RG
Tel. 071 821 1313
Hours: 10am-5.50pm Mon-Sat,
2-5.50pm Sun. Closed Good Friday,
May Day, Dec 24-26, Jan 1.

Saatchi Collection
98A Boundary Road,
London NW8 0RH
Tel. 071 624 8299
Hours: Fri and Sat 12-6pm.

Tate Gallery, Liverpool
Albert Dock, Liverpool L3 4BB
Tel. 051 709 3223
Hours: April-Sept: Tues-Sun 11-
7pm; Oct-March: Tues-Fri 11-5pm,
weekends 11-6pm.

Whitworth Art Gallery
Oxford Road, Manchester M15 6ER
Tel. 061 273 4865
Hours: Mon-Sat 10am-5pm, Thurs
10am-9pm.

Sainsbury Centre
Earlham Road, Norwich,
Norfolk NR4 7TJ
Tel. 0603 56060
Hours: Tues-Sun 12-5pm.

Southampton City Art Gallery
Civic Centre, Southampton SO9 4XF
Tel. 0703 832769
Hours: Tues-Fri 10am-5pm, Sat
10am-4pm, Sun 2-5pm, Thurs 6-
8pm (seasonal).

● Ireland

**The Hugh Lane Municipal Gallery
of Modern Art**
Charlemont,
Parnell Square, Dublin 1
Tel. 0001 741903
Hours: Tues-Sat 9.30-5pm, Sun 11-
5pm. Closed Mon.

● Italy

**Galeria d'Arte Moderne
di Palazzo Pitti**
Piazza Pitti 1, 50125 Florence
Tel. 55 287096
Hours: Tues-Sat 9am-2pm, Sun
9am-1pm. Closed Mon.

**Civico Museo d'Arte
Contemporanea**
Piazzo Duomo 14, 20121 Milan
Tel. 2 62083156
Hours: Tues-Sun 9.30am-12.30pm
and 2.30-5.20pm. Closed Mon.

**Galleria Nazionale d'Arte
Moderna-Arte Contemporanea**
Viale delle Belle Arti 131, 00197 Rome
Tel. 6 802751
Hours: Tues-Sat 9am-2pm, Sun
9am-1pm. Closed Mon.

**Museo Galleria d'Arte
Moderna**
Ca'Pesaro, Canal Grande, 30100
Venice
Tel. 41 5241075
Hours: daily 9am-7pm. Closed Mon.

**Fondazione
Peggy Guggenheim**
Palazzo Venier dei Leoni, 701
Dorsoduro, 30123 Venice
Tel. 41 520 6288
Hours: Wed-Fri and Sun-Mon 11am-
6pm, Sat noon-9pm. Closed Tues.

● Mexico

Museo de Frida Kahlo
Londres 127, Coyoacan,
Mexico City
Tel. 525 5545999
Hours: Tues-Sun 10am-6pm. Closed
Mon.

Museo de Arte Moderno
Bosque de Chapultepec, paseo de la
Reforma y Gandhi, 11560 Mexico,
047 DF
Tel. 5 554 5999
Hours: Tues-Sun 10am-6pm.
Closed Mon.

Museo del Palacio de Bellas Artes
Ave Juarez y Angela Peralta,
Mexico City 06050
Tel. 5 512 3633
Hours: Tues-Sun 10.30am-6.30pm.
Closed Mon.

● The Netherlands

Rijkmuseum Vincent van Gogh
Paulus Pottersraat 7, 1071 CX
Amsterdam
Tel. 20 764881
Hours: 10am-5pm Tues-Sat, 1-5pm
Sun and holidays. Closed Mon and
Jan 1.

Stedelijk Museum
Paulus Pottersraat 13, 1071 CX
Amsterdam
Tel. 20 5732911 or 5732737
Hours: daily 11am-5pm, Sun and
holidays 1-5pm.

Stedelijk van Abbe-Museum
Bilderdijklaan 10, 5611 NH
Eindhoven
Tel. 40 389730
Hours: Tues-Sat 10am-5pm, Sun
and holidays 1-5pm. Closed Mon.

Haags Gemeentemuseum
Stadhouderslaan 41, PO Box 72,
2501 CB The Hague
Tel. 70 3514181
Hours: Tues-Sat 10am-5pm.
Closed Mon.

Rijkmuseum Kroller-Muller
De Hoge Veluwe National Park,
Otterlo
Tel. 8382 241
Hours: from April to Oct: Tues-Sat

10am-5pm, Sun and holidays 11am-
5pm. Nov to March: Tues-Sat 10am-
5pm, Sun and holidays 1-5pm.
Closed Mon.

● New Zealand

Auckland City Art Gallery
POB 5449, Auckland 1
Tel. 9 792 020
Hours: Mon-Thurs 10am-4.30pm,
Fri to 8.30pm, Sat and Sun 1-
5.30pm.

National Art Gallery
Buckle Street, POB 467, Wellington
Tel. 4 859 703
Hours: daily 10am-4.45pm.

● Norway

Nasjonalgalleriet
Universtitetsgaten 13, 0164 Oslo 1
Tel. 2 20 04 04
Hours: Mon, Wed, Fri and Sat
10am-4pm, Thurs 10am-8pm, Sun
11am-3pm. Closed Tues and
national holidays.

Munch-Museet
Toyengaten 53, 0578 Oslo 5
Tel. 2 67 37 74
Hours: Tues-Sat 10am-8pm, Sun
noon-8pm. Closed Mon and
national holidays.

Museet for Samtidskunst (National Museum of Contemporary Art)
Bankplassen 4, 0151 Oslo 1
Tel. 2 53 49 81
Hours: Tues-Fri 11am-7pm, Sat-Sun
11am-4pm. Closed Mon and
national holidays.

Heine-Onstad Kunstsenter
Sonja Henievs. 31, Blommenholm,
1311
Hovikodden
Tel. 2 54 30 50
Hours: Mon 11am-5pm, Tues-Fri
9am-9pm, Sat-Sun 11am-7pm.
Closed national holidays.

● Spain

Fundacion "Joan Miró"
Parque Montjuich, 08004 Barcelona
Tel. 3 329 1908
Hours: Tues-Sat 11am-8pm, Sun
and national holidays 11am-
2.30pm.

Museo de Arte Moderno
Parque de la Ciudadela, 08003
Barcelona
Tel. 3 310 6308 or 319 5728
Hours: Tues-Sun 9am-7.30pm, Mon
3-7.30pm, national holidays 9am-
2pm.

Museo Picasso
Calle de Montcada 15-17, 08003
Barcelona
Tel. 93 319 6310 or 319 6902
Hours: daily 9am-2pm and 4-
8.30pm. Closed Sun afternoon and
Mon.

Museo Dalí
Plaza Gala y Salvador Dalí, 5 17600
Figueras-Gerona
Tel. 972 50-5697
Hours: daily 10.30am-noon, 3.30-
7pm. Closed Mon, Christmas Day
and New Year's Day.

Museo del Prado "Cason del Buen Retiro"
Paseo Prado s/n, 28014 Madrid
Tel. 91 468 0481
Hours: from Oct 16-May 15, 9am-
6.30pm; rest of year, 9am-7pm. Sun
10am-2pm. Closed Mon and
national holidays.

Museo Espanol de Arte Contemporaneo
Avenida Juan de Herrera 2, 28040
Madrid
Tel. 91 449 2453 or 449 7150
Hours: daily 10am-6pm, Aug 10am-
2pm. Closed Mon.

● Sweden

Moderna Museet
Skeppsholmen, Box 16382, 10327
Stockholm
Tel. 8 666 42 50
Hours: Tues-Fri 11am-9pm, Sat and
Sun 11am-5pm. Closed Mon.

● Switzerland

Öffentlicher Kuntsammlung Basel Kuntsmuseum
St Alban-Graben 16,
4010 Basel
Tel. 61 22 08 28
Hours: Tues-Sun 10am-5pm. Closed
Mon, Christmas Day, New Year's
Day and local holidays.

Kuntsmuseum
Hodlerstraase 8-12, 3011 Bern
Tel. 31 220944
Hours: Tues 10am-9pm, Wed-Sun
10am-5pm. Closed Mon, Christmas
Day, New Year's Day and local
holidays.

Petit Palais (Musée d'Art Moderne)
2 Terrasse Saint-Victor, Geneva
Tel. 22 46 1433
Hours: daily 10am-noon, 2am-6pm.
Closed Mon morning, Christmas
Day, New Year's Day and local
holidays.

Kunsthaus
Heimplatz 1, 8024 Zurich
Tel. 1 251 67 65
Hours: Mon 2-5pm, Tues-Fri 10am-
9pm, weekends 10am-5pm. Closed
Christmas Day, New Year's Day and
local holidays.

● USA

Museum of Fine Arts
465 Huntington Ave, Boston, MA
02115
Tel. 617 267 9300
Hours: Tues, Thurs-Sun 10am-5pm,
Wed 10am-10pm. Closed Mon,
Christmas Eve and Day, New Year's
Day, July 4.

Albright-Knox Art Gallery
1285 Elmwood Avenue, Buffalo, NY
14222
Tel. 716 882 8700
Hours: Tues-Sat 11am-5pm, Sun 12-
5pm. Closed Mon, Thanksgiving,
Christmas, New Year's Day.

The Art Institute of Chicago
Michigan Ave at Adams Street,
Chicago, IL 60603
Tel. 312 443 3600
Hours: Mon-Wed 10.30am-4.30pm,
Thurs 10.30am-8pm, Fri 10.30am-
4.30pm, Sat 10.30am-5pm, Sun
and national holidays 12-5pm.
Closed Christmas Day.

Museum of Contemporary Art
250 South Grand Ave, California
Plaza, Los Angeles, CA 90012
Tel. 213 621 2766
Hours: Tues-Sun 11am-6pm, Thurs

11am-8pm. Closed Mon and public
holidays.

The Barnes Foundation
Box 128, Merion Station, PA 19066
Tel. 215 667 0290
Hours: Fri and Sat 9.30am-4.30pm,
Sun 1-4.30pm. Closed national
holidays. Numbers restricted, so
worth reserving by telephone.

Metropolitan Museum of Art
Fifth Avenue at 82nd Street, New
York, NY 10028
Tel. 212 535 7710
Hours: Tues 10am-8.45pm, Wed-
Sat 10am-4.45pm, Sun and national
holidays 11am-4.45pm. Closed
Mon, Thanksgiving, Christmas Day,
New Year's Day.

MoMA (Museum of Modern Art)
18 West 54th Street, New York, NY
10019
Tel: 212 708 9400
Hours: daily 11am-6pm, Thurs
11am-9pm. Closed Wed.

S.R. Guggenheim Museum
1071 Fifth Avenue at 88th Street,
New York, NY 10028
Tel. 212 860 1313
Hours: Wed-Sun 11am-5pm, Tues
11am-8pm. Closed Mon.

Whitney Museum of American Art
945 Madison Ave at 75th Street,
New York, NY 10021
Tel. 212 570 3600
Hours: Tues 11am-8pm, Wed-Sat
11am-6pm, Sun and national
holidays 12-6pm. Closed Mon.

Philadelphia Museum of Art
Benjamin Franklin Parkway,
Philadelphia, PA 19101
Tel. 215 763 8100
Hours: Wed-Sun 10am-5pm. Closed
Mon, Tues and national holidays.

San Francisco Museum of Modern Art
Van Ness at McAllister, San
Francisco, CA 94102
Tel. 415 863 8800
Hours: Tues, Wed and Fri 10am-
6pm, Thurs 10am-10pm, Sat and
Sun 10am-5pm. Closed Mon and
national holidays.

Hirshhorn Museum and Sculpture Garden
Smithsonian Institute, Independence
Avenue at 8th Street SW,
Washington, DC 20560
Tel. 202 357 1618
Hours: daily 10am-5.30pm, closed
Christmas Day. Extended summer
hours decided each year. Sculpture
garden open 7.30am-dusk.

National Museum of Women in the Arts
1250 New York Ave NW,
Washington, DC 20005
Tel. 202 783 5000
Hours: Mon-Sat 10am-5pm, Sun
12-5pm.

The Phillips Collection
1600-1612 21st Street NW,
Washington, DC 20009
Tel. 202 387 2151
Hours: Tues-Sat 10am-5pm, Sun 2-
7pm. Closed Mon and some
national holidays.

● USSR

State Hermitage Museum
Dvortsovaya nab. 34, Leningrad
191065
Tel. 7 812 212 9545
Hours: Tues-Fri 10.30am-6.30pm,
Sat-Sun 10am-6pm. Closed Mon.

State Tretyakov Gallery
Lavrushinski per. 10, Moscow
109017
Tel. 7 095 231 13 62
Hours: Tues-Sun 10am-7pm. Closed
Mon.

State Russian Museum,
Ulitsa Inhenernaya ul. 4, Leningrad
Tel. 7 812 314 41 53
Hours: daily 10am-6pm. Closed
Tues.

BOOKS ON MODERN ART

If this book has whetted your appetite and made you want to find out more about modern art, the following book list will point you in the right direction.

● General

Concepts of Modern Art
Nikos Stangos (ed.)
Thames and Hudson

Modern Art: A Graphic Guide
Dave Clarke and Julie Hollings
Camden Press, London
(Not available in the U.S.A.)

The Oxford Companion to
Twentieth Century Art
Henry Osborne (ed.)
Oxford University Press

The Shock of the New: Art and the
Century of Change
Robert Hughes
BBC Publications
(Published in the U.S.A. under the
imprint McGraw-Hill)

The Story of Art
E.H. Gombrich
Phaidon

A World History of Art
Hugh Honour and John Fleming
Macmillan

The Story of Modern Art
Norbert Lynton
Phaidon

The Thames and Hudson Dictionary
of Art Terms
Edward Lucie-Smith
Thames and Hudson

Theories of Modern Art
Herschel B. Chipp
University of California Press

Ways of Seeing
John Berger
BBC Publications & Penguin Books

Women, Art and Society
Whitney Chadwick
Thames and Hudson

● Movements

Abstract Art
Anna Moszynska
Thames and Hudson

Abstract Expressionism
David Anfam
Thames and Hudson

Bauhaus
Frank Whitford
Thames and Hudson

Cubism
Edward F. Fry
Thames and Hudson

Dada: Art and Anti-Art
Hans Richter
Thames and Hudson

The Expressionists
Wolf-Dieter Dube
Thames and Hudson

Fauvism
Sarah Whitfield
Thames and Hudson

Futurism
Caroline Tisdale and Angelo Bozolla
Thames and Hudson

Impressionism
Phoebe Pool
Thames and Hudson

Pop Art
Lucy Lippard et al
Thames and Hudson

The Post-Impressionists
Belinda Thomson
Phaidon
(Published in the U.S.A. under the
imprint School Living)

The Russian Experiment in Art
1863 - 1922
Camilla Gray
Thames and Hudson

Surrealism
Patrick Waldberg
Thames and Hudson

Symbolist Art
Edward Lucie-Smith
Thames and Hudson

● Selected artists

Francis Bacon
John Russell
Thames and Hudson

Braque
Serge Fauchereau
Academy Editions
(Published in the U.S.A. under the
imprint Rizzoli International)

Paul Cézanne
Hajo Duchting
Benedikt Taschen
(Not available in the U.S.A.)

Marc Chagall: Gouaches, Drawings,
Watercolours
Werner Haftmann
Thames and Hudson
(Published in the U.S.A. by Harry N.
Abrams, Inc.)

Salvador Dalí
Dawn Ades
Thames and Hudson
(Not available in the U.S.A.)

Willem de Kooning
Diane Waldman
Thames and Hudson
(Not available in the U.S.A.)

Georgia O'Keeffe
Lisa Minz Messinger
Thames and Hudson, and
Metropolitan
Museum of Art, NY

A Life of Picasso: Vol. 1: 1881-1906
John Richardson
Jonathan Cape

● Selected artists (continued)

Picasso
Timothy Hilton
Thames and Hudson

Jackson Pollock: An American Saga
Steve Naifeh and Gregory White
Smith
Barrie and Jenkins
(Not available in the U.S.A.)

The Rodchenko Family Workshop
Serpentine Gallery, London:
exhibition catalogue
(Not available in the U.S.A.)

Van Gogh
Melissa McQuillan
Thames and Hudson

Andy Warhol
Carter Ratcliff
Abbeville Press

● Museum guides

Amsterdam Art Guide
Christian Reinwald
A & C Black
(Not available in the U.S.A.)

The Art Galleries of Britain and
Ireland: A Guide to their Collections
Joan Abse
Robson Books
(Published in America by Fairleigh
Dickenson University Press)

Art in America: Annual Guide to
Museums, Galleries & Artists
Brant Art Publications Inc, NY

Australian Arts Guide
Roslyn Keane
A & C Black
(Not available in the U.S.A.)

Berlin Arts Guide
Irene Blumenfeld
A & C Black
(Not available in the U.S.A.)

Blue Guide: Museums and Galleries
of London
Malcolm Rogers
A & C Black
(Published in the U.S.A. under the
imprint W.W. Norton)

Glasgow Arts Guide
Alice Bain
A & C Black
(Not available in the U.S.A.)

London Art and Artists Guide
Heather Waddell
A & C Black
(Not available in the U.S.A.)

Madrid Arts Guide
Claudia Oliveira
A & C Black
(Not available in the U.S.A.)

The Mitchell Beazley Travellers'
Guides to Art: Britain and Ireland
Michael Jacobs and Paul Stirton
Mitchell Beazley
(Not available in the U.S.A.)

The Mitchell Beazley Travellers'
Guides to Art: France
Michael Jacobs and Paul Stirton
Mitchell Beazley
(Not available in the U.S.A.)

New York Art Guide
Deborah Jane Gardner
A & C Black
(Published in the U.S.A. under the
imprint Art Guide Publications)

Paris Art Guide
Fiona Dunlop
A & C Black
(Not available in the U.S.A.)

Simon and Schuster Pocket Art
Museum Guide
Mitchell Beazley
(Out of print in the U.S.A. Formerly
published by Prentice Hall Press)

● Art as a living

Making Art Pay
Bernard Denvir and Howard Gray
Phaidon
(Not available in the U.S.A.)

Making Ways: The Visual Arts Guide
to Surviving and Thriving
David Butler (ed.)
Artic Producers Publishing Co. Ltd
(Not available in the U.S.A.)

Magazines

Great Britain

Art Monthly

Artscribe International

Modern Painters

Artrage

USA

Art News

Art Forum

Art in America

Australia

Art and Australia

Art Monthly

New Zealand

Art New Zealand

GLOSSARY AND INDEX

Glossary

Abstract art: non-representational art. That is, art which does not try to represent people, animals or objects in the real world, but which attempts to communicate meaning either through dramatically simplified or invented forms.

Avant-garde: artists who pioneer new approaches, styles or techniques in defiance of the establishment. The term derives from "vanguard", meaning the leading unit in an army.

Figurative art: also known as representational art. It depicts recognizable (though not necessarily realistic) people, animals or objects. The opposite of abstract art.

Fine art: collective term to describe painting, sculpture, drawing and printmaking and sometimes also music and poetry. The main difference between fine and applied or decorative arts (such as pottery or embroidery) is that fine arts serve no practical purpose.

Found object: a naturally-occurring or man-made object, such as driftwood, fabric or a bottle which, unaltered, is either exhibited as an artistic object in its own right, or incorporated into a work of art.

Frottage: French for "rubbing". A design made by placing paper over a textured surface and rubbing it with a pencil or crayon to produce an impression of the surface on the paper.

Old master: one of the celebrated European painters of the period c1400-1800, or a painting by one of them.

Perspective: in painting, a convention used to convey the illusion of three dimensions on a flat surface, mainly by making parallel lines appear to converge as they recede from the viewer and by making subjects appear to diminish in size, the further they are from the foreground of the painting.

Plein air: a principle of Impressionism. The Impressionists tried to capture the fleeting moment in their work. As they often painted outdoor scenes, they chose the term "plein air" (meaning open air) both to describe the situation in which they painted and the atmosphere which they tried to convey in their work.

Ready-made: name given by Marcel Duchamp to a manufactured object, such as a bicycle wheel or a bottle-rack, which he chose, at random, to exhibit as a work of art.

Renaissance: a period of cultural rebirth in Europe during the 15th and 16th centuries inspired by the art and learning of ancient Greece and Rome.

Index

Acknowledgements

Pages 2-3: cartoon: (Snap! Bop! Crunch!) by Heath, © 1967 Punch; Golub photo courtesy of the artist; mural courtesy Graham Cooper; Niki de Saint Phalle, photo by Laurent de Condominos, courtesy Gimpel Fils, London; Persil, courtesy J. Walter Thompson; cartoon (Miss Angelo) by Starke, © 1948 Punch; Rietveld chair, photo courtesy Barry Friedman Ltd; Cézanne, Musée d'Orsay, Paris, photograph © R.M.N.; café photo courtesy Roger Viollet.

Pages 4-5: Pollock, Tate Gallery, London, © 1990 Pollock-Krasner Foundation/ARS, NY; photo of Pollock © Hans Namuth 1990; cartoons: ("Willy") Evening News, Associated Newspapers Group Ltd., © 1936, by Lee; ("His spatter is masterful") by Peter Arno, © 1953, 1981 The New Yorker Magazine Inc.

Pages 6-7: Cézanne, Musée d'Orsay, Paris, photo © R.M.N.; Braque, Tate Gallery, London © ADAGP and DACS, London 1991; O'Keeffe, The Metropolitan Museum of Art, the Alfred Stieglitz Collection, 1952, © 1990 The Estate and Foundation of Georgia O'Keeffe/ARS, NY; cartoon, by Bruce Cavalier, London Opinion, 1953.

Pages 8-9: Monet, The Museum of Modern Art, New York, Mrs Simon Guggenheim Fund, © DACS 1991; Van Gogh, The Museum of Modern Art, New York, acquired through the Lillie P. Bliss Bequest; Matisse, Tate Gallery, London, succession H. Matisse/DACS 1991; photos: Giverny courtesy French Government Tourist Office; snail, ZEFA Picture Library; cartoon, Le Charivari, 1877 by CHAM.

Pages 10-11: Miró, The Museum of Modern Art, New York, Purchase, © ADAGP, Paris and DACS, London 1991; Moore, Tate Gallery, London, © Henry Moore Foundation, 1991, reproduced by kind permission of the Henry Moore Foundation; de Kooning, The Museum of Modern Art, New York, Purchase, © DACS, 1991; photo (pin-up), The Kobal Collection; cartoon: Punch, 27 June 1951.

Pages 12-13: Chagall, The Museum of Modern Art, New York, acquired through the Lillie P. Bliss Bequest, © ADAGP, Paris and DACS, London 1991; photo: Roger Viollet; cartoon: Fliegende Blatter, 2 Dec. 1898, by A. Roeseler; Lehmbruck, Staatsgalerie Moderner Kunst, Munich, photo by Artothek.

Pages 14-15: Picasso, The Museum of Modern Art, New York, The Sidney and Harriet Janis Collection, © DACS 1991; Seurat, Berggruen Collection, on loan to the National Gallery, London; Kahlo, reproduction authorized by Instituto Nacional De Bellas Artes Y Literatura; photo (Kahlo and Rivera) Peter A. Juley & Son Collection, National Museum of American Art, Smithsonian Institution, Washington; cartoon, Punch, 25 Feb. 1948 by Starke.

Pages 16-17: Delaunay, Emanuel Hoffman-Stiftung, Kunstmuseum, Basel, Colorphoto Hans Hinz, © ADAGP, Paris and DACS, London 1991; Giacometti, Peggy Guggenheim Collection, Venice, The Solomon R. Guggenheim Foundation, Photo by David Heald, © ADAGP, Paris and DACS, London 1991; Dubuffet, from the Paris Circus series, 1961, The Museum of Modern Art, New York, Mrs Simon Guggenheim Fund, © ADAGP, Paris and DACS, London 1991; photos: film still, BFI, © Transit-Film Gesellschaft MBH; Eiffel Tower, ZEFA Picture Library; Graffiti, ZEFA Picture Library.

Pages 18-19: Balla, Albright-Knox Gallery, Buffalo, New York, Bequest of A. Conger Goodyear and Gift of George F. Goodyear, 1964; Victory of Samothrace © Photo R.M.N.; photos: chronograph, Science Museum, London; racing car, Quadrant Photo Library; Op art, Camera Press.

Pages 20-21: Blume, The Museum of Modern Art, New York, Mrs Simon Guggenheim Fund; Golub, courtesy of the artist; Grosz, photo Jörg P. Anders, Berlin, © DACS 1991; photo: Blackshirts, Popperfoto.

Pages 22-23: Willrich, Weimar Archive; photos: Agit Prop train, Society for Cultural Relations with USSR; Goebbels, Weimar Archive; cartoon: Jugend 1933 by Garvens.

Pages 24-25: Wyndham Lewis, Trustees of the Imperial War Museum; Picasso, © DACS 1991; photos: Soldiers, Imperial War Museum; Guernica, Camera Press.

Pages 26-27: Rousseau, The Museum of Modern Art, New York, Gift of Mrs Simon Guggenheim; Dalí, The Museum of Modern Art, New York, given anonymously © DEMART PRO ARTE BV/DACS, London 1991; Ernst, Tate Gallery, London, © ADAGP, Paris and DACS, London 1991; photo: Dalí, Edimedia; cartoons: Surrealist Family by Carl Rose, © 1937, 1965 The New Yorker Magazine, Inc.; Dalí by John Art Sibley, Strand 1946.

Pages 28-29: Chagall, gift of Alfred S. Alschuler, 1946.925, photo © 1990, The Art Institute of Chicago, all rights reserved, © ADAGP, Paris and DACS, London 1991; African sculpture, Werner Forman Archive; photo: Weimar Archive.

Pages 30-31: Gauguin, Tomkins Collection, courtesy Museum of Fine Arts, Boston; Kandinsky, Tate Gallery, London © ADAGP, Paris and DACS, London 1991; photo: Cossacks, Weimar Archive.

Pages 32-33: Duchamp © ADAGP, Paris and DACS, London 1991; Picasso © photo R.M.N.; photos: Arnatt, courtesy The Photographers' Gallery, London; Brisley, courtesy of the artist, photo by Brian Marsh.

Pages 34-35: murals courtesy Graham Cooper and Doug Sargent; Niki de Saint Phalle, photo by Laurent Condominos, courtesy Gimpel Fils, London; Chicago, © Judy Chicago, 1979, photo by Donald Woodman; photo Barnaby's Picture Library.

Pages 36-37: Mondrian © DACS 1991; photos: Schroder House, Utrecht Tourist Office; chairs and lamp, Barry Friedman Ltd; Café, Les Musées de Ville de Strasbourg; sportswear, photo Serpentine Gallery; Bauhaus, Weimar Archive; Club, Society for Cultural Relations with USSR.

Pages 38-39: Lichtenstein © DACS 1991; Warhol © 1990 The Estate and Foundation of Andy Warhol/ARS, NY; photos: Marilyn Monroe, Camera Press; Persil, J. Walter Thompson; Boots, CDP & Partners Ltd; The Animation Partnership.

Pages 40-41: Nam June Paik courtesy Holly Solomon Gallery.

Pages 42-43: Andre © DACS 1991; photo of auction, courtesy Christie's; cartoon © Calman.

Pages 44-45: photos: Café and Bateau Lavoir, Roger Viollet; Gertrude Stein, The Beinecke Rare Book and Manuscript Library, Yale University; cartoon by Koren, © 1968, The New Yorker Magazine Inc.

First published in 1991 by Usborne Publishing Ltd, Usborne House, 83-85 Saffron Hill, London EC1N 8RT, England.

Printed in Scotland.